T0142456

GALAXIES:
FAREWELL EARTH

C. L. FRAZIER

author<small>HOUSE</small>

AuthorHouse™
1663 Liberty Drive
Bloomington, IN 47403
www.authorhouse.com
Phone: 833-262-8899

Published by AuthorHouse 05/09/2022

ISBN: 978-1-6655-5948-5 (sc)
ISBN: 978-1-6655-5947-8 (e)

Print information available on the last page.

This book is printed on acid-free paper.

CONTENTS

CHAPTER 1

The room was dim-lit and filled with hundreds of electronics with blinking lights. Four eighty-inch flat-screen computer monitors surround the room just above several control panels. Each screen contained radar sequences from North, South, East, and West of the directional satellite feed. A young man in his early twenties' sleeps while sitting in a computer chair halfway laying on one of the control panels. A slight beeping alarm awakens him from his deep and needed slumber as he arises in a fright at the sudden noise.

The young man jumps from his chair causing it to spin to the back of the room as he looks at the monitors but finds no trace of movement. Confused at the alarm and dazed from his slumber, he types in a few codes and a recording popped up onto the screen. When he presses play, a raspy voice comes over the monitor with a familiar yet unknown language. The mysterious message lasts for about five minutes and then ends with dead silence. Excitedly, the man rushes to copy the message onto a USB drive and runs out of the monitoring room with a grin.

He runs down the long hallway to the elevator and presses the button for the first floor. After impatiently waiting for the elevator to stop, he runs down another hall to the primary office and bursts through his boss's door. The older pot-bellied man behind the desk jumps with a startle at the sudden intrusion.

"SIR!" the young nerd shouts out of breath. "You have got to hear this! We picked up something strange."

He reveals the USB drive and places it on his bosses' desk sliding it over to him. The office was small with a single computer desk with many military plaques and rewards covering the walls. On the desk lay a closed laptop, a stack of files, and an office phone. The pugly man behind the desk was a Sergeant in the military in his late forties. Annoyed with the sudden interruption, he sets a file down onto the desk.

"This had better be good." He said with a scowl.

The young satellite tech sat nervously into the chair as his boss placed the USB drive into the laptop and brought up the only file. After the mysterious message stopped playing, the Sergeant rubbed his eyes as he thought about it.

"Sounds a little like German." The Sergeant finally said. "Did we pick up on any of their feed?"

"No sir." The tech replied. "There are no German satellites in the Eastern rotation, I checked."

"Then I'll send this to a translator, and have it sent to intelligence once it's finished."

Still excited at his find but disappointed in the reaction, the young tech left the room and headed back to the monitor room. The Sergeant was rusty on his German, but what words he could make out was enough to make him break out in a cold sweat as he sent the email.

In a small collage dorm in Washington, a young student sat down at her laptop to study as her email pinged in. She was in her mid-twenties and going through her senior year to be a translator over seas. She had translated a few things throughout her time for some quick cash and was excited to see a request in her email. As she pulled up the email, a small message was attached with limited details.

Please translate this German message and send it to Millitary Intelligence in the link below for further action.
Thank you, Sgt. Recker

She scrolled to the bottom of the email and clicked the message attachment, excitedly. A five-minute-long audio message began to play as she listened carefully to every word. As the message played, her smile became a frown and her heart began to race with fear. She quickly saved the file to her laptop and began translating each word as she reloaded the terrifying message.

After finishing the translation, she attached the new audio message to an email and sent it to Military Intelligence as requested. She carefully closed her email and the laptop then ran out of her dorm in tears as she called her family. As she ran from the building and waiting for someone to pick up, the only thought in her mind was that the millitary could not help. To her, there was no fighting this or hope for anyone at this point in time. It wouldn't be long before her and everyone else's world would be crashing down around them.

In Washington D.C., a large three-story building sat on two blocks of property near the edge of the city. The name of the building read:

Central Intelligence Agency C.I.A

Inside a small office on the third floor sat a six-foot four tall full blood Cherokee man at the age of thirty-two. His dark hair met his lower back as it was tied and braded into a long ponytail. Born and raised on a Native American Reservation, he was the second son of the Chief and pride of his people.

The day of his eighteenth birthday, he announced that he would be setting out to join the U.S Millitary. In the last fourteen years, he had done three tours in Afghanistan and two tours in Iran. He was then Honorably Discharged with a Purple Heart after being shot in the chest during his last tour in Iran while saving his Platoon of twenty men and women. Within the first eight years of his millitary career, he went from the rank of Private, to Commanding Officer.

He gained the rank of Commander after earning his Purple Heart and recived an office in the C.I.A. For the last six years, the Commander has worked in Washington D.C. with his own team of agents. His job was to resolve millitary disputes and gather intel from apprehended war criminals. The man's name, is Commander Waya Aholoke.

He was filing documents of his most recent case when the email popped up on his laptop. Inside was a five-minute audio message from one of the translators under his payroll. She was relatively new and was from California. She was here in Washington for college. Just like the many messages he has went through before, he retrieved his pen and notebook then clicked play. He did not write anything down for the duration of the myserious audio message. Instead, he stared at the screen in shock as his heart-rate sped up from fear and anger with every horrifying word.

Growing up on the Cherokee reservation, he had learned a great deal about the sins of the outside world. His entire life's dream was to stop the maddness of the world and bring the people together. Though he knew about the horrors of the past, he did not hold a grudge against those who call America home now. He knew that people learned from their history and better themselves, as he has through his years in the military. After listening to this message of fate, he knew that the world may have no choice but to follow those life-long dreams.

Thirty-two years of his life he has never lied or hid anything from his superiors for any reason. For thirty-two years he has never disobeyed a direct order from even his elders or others he looked up to. All of this raced through his mind as he downloaded the audio message and deleted the email. This would be his one and only hidden secret from his superiors as he shut off his laptop and left the room. All he could think about was that this could be his chance to make a difference in the world like he has always dreamed of doing.

Learning about the outside world while he grew up, he knew that the only way to accomplish his dream was through power as everyone else had. Throughout his fourteen- year military career, he had made many powerful friends. It was time to cash in and make his dreams a reality, but he would need to be smart on who to trust. There were a few that he could think of, but ony a small handful. It was time for Commandor Waya Aholoke to visit these friends.

The young woman was pretty wih her long wavy red hair and pasty white skin with noticable freckles above her nose. At the age of thirty, she is two years fresh out of college and has made the rank of Vice President in the White House. She is young but smart and was hand-picked by the running president to stand at his side. He noticed her grades were exponential in all subjects the day she applied for a basic political job. She had more potential than she was showing and he couldn't pass up the opportunity to challenge her skills. On top of that, seeing her background of all the things she had done for the community, Aine O'Conner was the perfect choice for the job.

Waya Aholoke appeared in her office doorway as she was about to leave for lunch. Her face lit up brightly as their eyes met, as they have done many times before. They had met a year before when she was first assigned the job of Vice President and he was her bodyguard.

"Long time, no see stranger." Aine said shyly. "What's it been now? About two weeks?"

"I….. Have been busy." Waya replied, embarrassed.

When they had met the year before, Aine saw him as a rough and frightening soldier. But as they talked and got to know each other better, when on their private plane rides, her view of him had changed. He was her escort bodyguard for six weeks before they had began dating. Their jobs made it hard to see each other as much as they wanted to, but they always made it work.

"I see you're about to go to lunch." He said teasingly, knowing when she always leaves. "May I join you?"

"You know you're always welcome." She replies flirtishly. "Of course you can, but you're paying."

"Don't I always?" He laughed.

"Only because you wont let me." She teases with a squint.

"What can I say?" He laughs. "I'm old fashion. Anyway, I'm glad to join you. We have a lot to discuss." His smile became a frown as he held up the USB drive. Now she knew this was not just a normal pleasure visit.

CHAPTER 2

Miami, Florida was beautiful this time of year with sunny skies and steady cool winds. Families all over the city enjoyed the warm weather in the parks and at the beaches with their kids and pets. Down the street from a small community park was a two story three bedroom house that sat on a small patch of land. It was surrounded by a white picket fence with a two car garage beside it. In the back of the family home were two childern playing, a boy and a girl. The girl was six with short black frizzy hair and dark skin. The boy was nine with short black hair and dark skin as well, both siblings to a military family.

The kids' mother was watching them play from the patio when she heard a knock come from thr front of the house. She signaled her children to follow her as she entered the house to investigate the knock. The house was neat and clean with well organized pots and pans hanging above the kitchen island. In the livingroom, many pictures of her family hung on the walls. A few were of her husband in his military uiform, some with her and the kids and some solo.

She opened the door to a man with a familiar physique to her husband's with short black hair as dark as his skin. He was muscular even through his uniform and stood above her at least a full foot.

"Hey Ronny!" she said excitedly. "What brings you here? Come on in."

"Thanks Naya." He replied calmly and serious. "We need to talk. But not in front of the kids."

"Yeah, of course. Kids, head upstairs while Ronny and I talk." They both growned but complied. Her face became serious when she looked back at Ronny. "Okay, whats wrong?"

Ronny cleared his throat before he spoke. "It's about Eric and his platoon. They were ambushed by a group of unknown terrorists during a rally. Nobody survived… I'm sorry Naya."

Silence filled the room as Naya slowly walked to the mantle above the fireplace and took down a picture of her husband. She knew this was a risk from the day she met him, and she acceptrd it. But seeing it in the light after a decade together, she didn't know what to think. She held the picture of Eric tightly in her hands as she held back her tears. For the moment, the only sound in the house was from the kids playing upstairs.

"Don't worry Naya." Ronny said calmly. "I'll talk to a few people and make sure you and the kids are well taken care of.'

"Thank you Ronny." Naya replied with a bit of a wimper. "If you don't mind, I'd like to talk to the kids now."

All Ronny could do was nod silently and walk out the door for hr had nothing to say to comfort her. Once the door closed behind Ronny, Naya fell to her knees clutching her husband's picture in her hands and burst into tears. Out on the porch, Ronny could hear her crying and it angered him of her loss. Not only did she lose her husband and the kids their father, but Eric was his best friend and this was the only mission that they were not together for. They were originally supose to go on this simple rally mission together for a peace treaty, but he was needed elsewhere.

Ronny knew that he had to help them get taken care of because she and the kids would have to pack up and leave the safty of the base soon. He got into his two year old ford and activated the self-driving system as he set up the GPS. As the car drove towards his office, he used the touch-screen to contact his Commander. The phone rang three times before a man with a deep scratchy voice answered the call.

"Recruiters office, this is Commander Vice."

"Hey Commander, it's Ronny. How are things there?"

"Oh Ronny, things are good here. It's rare to hear from you. What can I do for you my boy?"

"I'll get right to the point. Sgt. Miller was killed in combat two days ago while on a rally mission and I was just informed."

"Hmmm I see. I'm sorry Ronny. I know you two were close. I take it you were the one to offered to notify his family."

"Yes, and I just left and I need a favor. I know this was his last tour and that they will have to leave the base soon now that he is gone. I want them taken care of."

"To be honest my boy, that is personal information I don't have acess to. Nor can I authorize such a request because it's above my pay grade. Every officer has a life insurance policy that she will now get."

"Her kids are young Commander, that money wont last long. I doubt it will even cover the burial."

"Look, Ronny there is a system to these things and legally I can't talk about a lot of it." There was a slight silence before Vice sighed. "Okay look, I have a meeting in Washington in a couple days. Come with me and talk to a few people. I can at least let her stay on base until we are back. And when you return for the funeral, maybe you will have what you are asking for. But no guarantees, these people are strict on all matters."

"Okay, I can do that. Thanks Vice." Ronny hung up the phone and thought of what he could do in Washington.

Naya hung up her phone with the Commander's office about the transfer of Eric's body. The kids sat on the couch in silence and sadness as their mother made preparations. Next, she dialed the funeral home in order to get details on dates, times, and prices. As she hung up, she got a call from her sister in law Angel, who was in tears.

"Hey sis." Angel cried. "I just heared. How are you all holding up?"

"We're managing." Naya replied. "Just called about his tranfer and funeral arrangements. His body will arrive in a couple days."

"Okay, that's good news. I talked to mama and we want to pay for the funeral. You need the insurance to live off of for awhile so you can get on your feet. We will help any way we can."

"Thanks Angel. Your name fits you well."

They shared a quick laugh and talked for several minutes about prices and dates. Within the hour, they said their goodbyes and hung up while still in tears about the unexpected happenings. Even thought Naya had many more places to call, it was too late in the day to do so. On top of that, she was too exhausted to do anything that has to do with Eric for the day.

CHAPTER 3

It was 10:05pm on the first night of summer in San Fancisco, California with a warm and relaxing breeze. Two cars were side by side in a street that was deserted within a three mile radius. Like many others in this major city, they were preparing to race for keeps as they revved their engines. One was a brand new 2037 Ford Mustang fresh off the lot with turbo engines and green-lighted rims. The body was blood red with snakes on each side, black in color, and a white skull with roses on the hood. Behind the wheel was a gangbanger in his twenties with tatoos up and down both arms and short brown hair.

The second car was a 2036 pure solid black Dodge Charger with turbo speed upgrades. The vehicle was plain but has been undeteated throughout the past six months with an unknown driver. Inside, the yet to be identified driver wore a leather jumpsuit and biker helmet. Not only have they not seen the driver's face, but they have not heared their voice throughout the entire six months. All around the two cars was a group of people watching and waiting in anticipation of the race to come.

In front of the two cars was a young woman in her early twenties wairing a tied up tank-top, short-shorts, and heels holding a red flag. As she waved the flag to signal the start of the race, the two drivers sped past her within seconds. They were side by side for the first three hundred feet until they neared the first curb in which the charger backed off a bit to drift. Taking his chance, the Mustang driver revved up and took the lead as her turned the corner. The myserious driver began to ride the tailwind of the Mustang and by the time he realized what was happening, he couldn't shake the Charger. Using his turbo dive to put some distance between them, the mustang driver sped around the next curb recklessly giving the unknown driver an unexpected lead with a drift.

With only a mile left to go, the mysterious charger driver used a turbo booster for the first time and put a great distance between the two racers. With fire blazing from the double muffler, the charger zoomed past the finish line in a flash. The crowd roared as the Charger slowed to a stop and the Mustang made its way to the finish line. The two racers shook hands as the crowd gathered around and the mysterious driver recived five grand for the win. After the exchange, a young man in his yearly twenties standing at five nine with long black hair to his sholders stepped forward. He wore a white tank top and ripped blue jeans with a Marine Corps tattoo on his right arm.

"So, you're the mysterious undefeated racer I've been hearing so much about." The man said with a slightly deep voice and the unknown driver just knotted. "I see it's true that you don't talk. I'd love to see what you're hiding under that helmet. What do you say to a little wager?" The concealed driver waved the five grand at the challanger. "I have something better than money in mind. If you win, you get my car." He pointed to the 2037 GTO in the nearby plaza.

"Boss don't, this guy is bad news…." The defeated racer began but was waved off by a hand.

"I know what I'm doing, unlike you and that pathetic race." The gang leader said. "Anyway, if I win then you have to take that helmet off and reveal yourself. After that you become my underling. What do you say? Got the balls newbie?"

The undefeated driver knotted in response after a moment of hesitation and got back into the Charger. The two racers parked at the same starting line as the last race as the croed watched in anticipation. The flagger took her position in front of the two vehicles as they revved up their engines. With a flick of a wrist, the flag waved to start the race and the two cars went fron zero to sixty within seconds and sped past the viewers. Taking the first curb with a slight drift, the Charger took the lead t the start for the first time.

The GTO was close behind and the undefeated slowed from 120MPH to only sisxy to keep the GTO in second. The gang leader watched as his opponent move for move to keep him in check and not give a tailwind to use. He could see why this driver was always undefeated due to not using the same tacic twice and using the opposing vehicle's power as an advantage. His first thought was that this was a veteran racer with years of experience. Every race had been recorded, as was his gang's policy to insure notes could be taken. He had reviewed every race that the myserious driver had been in and no two were the same.

Every strategy was different and every race was a fresh start with no mistakes and perfect precision. This driver had to be well known and professional in order to accomplish so much in such a short amout of time in street racing. Knowing that his gang was targeted and every one of them had been defeated, he was guessing that it had to be someone they knew and had defeated in the past. The only thing he could think of was this was revenge and this race would be the greatest. It was the only thing that made sense and would answer most of the questions that he had.

This driver had been taking over his territory for the past six months while he was on tour oer seas. During his time in the military, he was racing in the surrounding countries and making allies. From what he was told, this driver showed up just two days after he had left the country and has been causing quite the sceen. The timing was only more proof that this had to be someone from his past, most likely an enemy that was seeking revenge. This made him want to win the race even more and uncover who was causing so much trouble for his people.

From what he had seen in this and all the other races, there was only one way to win against this driver. It was a desperate move and a last resort that he hadn't tried in four years since he first started racing at seventeen. A fake-out ws his only hope of winning, but it was dagerouse for both him and his opponent. It had always worked to trick his opponent with both speed and direction while drifting. With only one mile to go, he had to make his move but he knew he would only have one shot.

He decided to slow to a complete stop as the Charger driver tookthe bait and slowed down to investigate. Not many people would take this kind of bait unless they had a kind heart that worried about others. He took his chance as the Charger slowed under 30MPH by kicking up his turbo and slamming on the gas. The GTO sped past the Charger within seconds, sending the driver into shock from the trickery. The mysterious driver punched the gas to catch up as they neared the last curb, but stayed in second place. By the time they had reached the final curb, the two racers were side by side and the Charger driver kicked the turbo in a final desperate attempt for the lead.

The undefeated driver stopped the turbo in order to slow down enough to side-swipe the tail end of the GTO. The reason was to send the GTO into a spin in order to take the led and win the race. With only a few feet to go, the Charger driver made the move but missed by just a few inched. Swerving in order to regain control, the Charger hit a car carrier truck ramp and went flying past the GTO. But losing control in mid-air caused the Charger to flip and land on its top as it slid across the road. The gang leader skid to a stop and watched as the Charger slid into a streetlight.

When there was no response from the other driver, he quickly got out of his GTO and rushed to his opponent's aid. Inside, the driver was hanging upside down and not moving as the specktators rushed over from the sidewalks. Everyone helped pry the door open and drag the unconscious driver to safty. After the driver was laid on the road, the gang leader felt his opponenet's chest for a heartbeat, but felt something weird. His mind raced with many thoughts and a tinge of fear sweped over him as he turned to his people.

"What the hell are you waiting for?" he yelled. "Call a damn ambulance!"

"Right, on it." One man replied. "You could have won the race first though."

"There is no honor in beating a dead racer."

He unzipped the driver's leather jacket to check if his opponent was still breathing as the ambulance made its way to them. As the sirens got closer, everyone scattered and left the two racers alone to deal with them. Shock filled the gang leader as he revealed the structure of a female body under the jacket. His heart pounded as he felt for a heartbeat and was glad that there was one, even though it was faint. He then quickly removed her helmet to give her air and hopped she was still breathing.

He sat beside her in shock at the site of her face as the ambulance pulled up, but was releaved she was alive. The medics wasted no time lifting her into the stretcher and put a breating mask over her nose and mouth. "Her long blond hair bounced as the medics hoisted the stretcher into the ambulance and closed the doors. As the ambulance drove down the street with its sirens on, the gang leader sat an the curb and thought about the last six months of her racing career. He couldn't understand how she could be so good at her young age knowing by her looks that she couldn't be more than fifteen or sixteen, just barely old enough to drive.

CHAPTER 4

It was early in the morning just after breakfast in Washington D.C. as three people sat in a conference room in the White House. The names of the conference attenders were Vice President Aine O'Conner, Commander Waya Aholoke, and Commander Ayden Vice. They sat at a large table, meant for thirty people, in silence as the translated audio message ended. For Waya this was his third time hearing it, yet it still gave him chills from the words that were spoken. It was the second time for Aine, who had her head down to hide the terror on her face. But for Ayden, this was his first time hearing the dredfull message and it sent chills through his entire body.

"So, any ideas or comments?" Waya asked, breaking the silence.

"Where did you get this Commander?" Ayden asked in response.

"NASA satellite monitors picked up the message and the one on duty gave it to his superior who sent it to a translator before it was sent to me directly as ordered."

"Where are they? And why aren't they at this meeting then? It would only be right to include them."

"Normally you would be right Commander." Aine chimed in. "But the man who had discovered the message cannot be found, and his superior is helping to locate him. The girl who had translated the message was soon put in a psychiatric facility after failing to commit suicide."

"Which is why we are having this meeting privately." Waya concluded. "We beleave that foul play was involved in the disappearance of the one who discovered the message."

"before we go public with this information, we need to come up with a plan to go about it quietly." Aine continued. "If foul play was involved, then we need to recruit only a small elite team that can help us announce this. Only some who can be trusted. Also, this could very well send the public into an anarchy rampage so we need to figure out the best way to let them know all at once and as gentally as we can."

"Honestly, how can we possibly tell anyone and make them believe?" Ayden asked. "Even I have a hard time believing it even with you announcing it. On top of that, what about those who have religious beliefs? Some would see this as fake news and others would see it as an apocalypse."

"They wouldn't be wrong." Aine interrupted with a mumble, forcing them both to stair at her. "What? It's true. The bible talks about fire raining down from the heavens at the start of the apocalypse. Technically, that will happen if we don't find a way to prevent it."

Okay, so how we tell the world all at once?" Waya asked. "And how do we prevent it from causing chaos and riots in the streets?in which would also cause a meltdow od civilization and curb the balance of power if it's not handled correctly."

"I know." Aine sighed. "So, me personally, I think we should stop holdng back secrets from the public. It causes too much speculation and disloyalty to the balance of power. I know that there are even secrets that even me and the President doesn't even know about. Like who the one who discovered the message disappeared. It only means that someone has leaked info and another powerful party doesn't want this revealed."

"What are you talking about?" Ayden asked. "You are the leaderes of this country. Don't tell me you believe that crap about secret government control and presidental figureheads."

"It's all true, and let me tell you why." Aine stood up and began to pase back and forth. "We are limited with time in our 'raign of power' so to speak. And for that, we are also limited to information. You wonder why we only get four to eight years of power yet many government officalls are in office for most of their lives? Someone is pulling strings. Those who tried to uncover them like JFK or Abe Lincoln, who were assasinated for such reasons."

"We all know that those two, like many others dug too deep." Waya chimed in. "For that, they were erased from exsistance. But they became symbles to the peope and for that, many laws and exceptions had to be met. In the end, the two got what they wanted. But it hasn't stopped the internal control. We must be quiet and swift about this. Otherwise, we will be the next on the chopping block."

"You mean to tell me that all those wack-job conspiracy theorist are right about closed door government secrets?" Ayden asked, standing up.

"That's correct." Aine replied. "And most likely they know about the message and want to cover it up for selfish reasons. It's also probably why the tech that discovered the message disappeared and the girl that translated it ended up getting addmited. There are holes in every story."

"If they know all that then they must know about this meeting!" Ayden was in a panic. "They could have traced our emails and calls."

"Trust me, they werent traced." Waya interrupted and put Ayden at ease. "Everything was secure with the codes that I personally designed. The group of people that I know and trust is small. So, can we trust you to help?"

"Help with what?" Aine said smiling. "But first we need to come up with a plan on how to go public secretly and unite the world when we do. So, what do you say Ayden? Are you with us?"

"I say you're all insane and complete idiots to go up against an invisable enemy. I'm in. Waya and I use to do this all the time until he got his Commander title. Now he's lazy." Ayden laughed a bit. "so, what's first on the list that we need to figure out?"

"You can start with who the guy outside the door is that you brought along with you." Waya suggested.

"Oh, that's Ronny Davis. I recruited him six years ago after you got your purple heart and was discharged. He reminded me a lot of you with being eager to learn and putting others needs before his own. His best friend was killed in action a few days ago from an ambush during a rally and is seeking help."

"You're talking about the truce rally ambush that killed fifteen people right?" Aine asked.

"That's the one." Ayden replied. "The man left behind a famiy with two kids under the age of ten. They live on base in Florida. Yoyu can guess his reasoning for being here. He wants to help, but is limited on what he can do. So I let him tag along to find some answers."

"And you trust him?" Aine asked Skeptically.

"With my life, as much as I do with Waya." Ayden said with a chuckle.

"I see. Then bring him in so we can talk to him. If you have that much trust in him, then so do we."

Outside the door, Ronny couldn't help but hear everything that was said in the small secret meeting. The audio message that he had heared was beyond frightening and sent shivers through his spine and made his hands sweat. Though the message was very real, all he could think of was that it couldn't be possible. The fact that his Commander was in league with the D.C. Commander and Vice President was more than overwheling. If that wasn't frightening enough, the fact that a ghost government was floating around controling peoples lives was.

How could they possibly keep this from a group of people with such resources and reveal this truth to the world while surviving the entire prosses were the questions that went through his mind. Ronny was snapped out of his thoughts when the conference room door opened and Ayden waved him in. As he walks in and looks around the room, he was directed to a chair beside Ayden after shaking hands with both Waya and Aine. Once the formalities were over, the conference room door closed and the meeting began.

CHAPTER 5

The flight back to Miami was relaxing after such a stressful meeting in D.C. with his Commander and the Vice President. There were many things that had to be done that day, including the funeral of his best friend of eight years. Before the plain had taken off for Florida, Ronny text a few trusted peole that he would 'like to catch up and discuss future plans'. After landing in Miami, he made his exit while replying to his texts for his busy week ahead. After texting Naya that he was on his way, he hauled his luggage into his car and made the seven mile drive to the funeral, which started in an hour.

Traffic was horrible and what would have only taken a few minutes, took over half han hour. Durring the drive, his mind flooded woth the meeting and everything that was said. The plans that Ayden, Waya and Aine had were beyond dangerous, but he agreed to them because the world needed to know. This would be his greatest and probably final mission as a Marine, a battle on the homefront against an invisable enemy. Naya and the kids were his first priority and he brought this to Anie's attention just before he left, and she agreed to his personal mission.

Ronny ha missed the service at the funeral home, but had made it to the burial just as it started. Soldiers in uniform stood in a line and began firing off shots in the air as a tribute to the fallen comrade. He made his way to the front and sat beside Naya and the kids who were trying to stay strong, but showed tears in their eyes. The casket was lowered into the ground as the shots continued in the sky and trumpets played. Everyone bowed their heads to pray for the lot soul s the burial and shots concluded. After the funeral, everyone gathered around the burial site to say their final goodbyes.

"You sure took your time getting here." Naya said with a playful irritation in her voice.

"Yeah, sorry." Ronny apologized. "I had some business to take care of in D.C."

"I take it that you just got back then? I'm glad you could make it. What did you have to do in D.C. that delayed you?"

"My Commander took me to a meeting with some federal people. That is really all I can say at the moment. I hope you understand." Ronny replied mournfully.

"Yeah, I understand. I went through that for six years now. Does that meeting mean that you are going to be deployed again?"

"Not overseas, but I will have quite a bit of traveling to do for awhile."

"When will you be leaving?" Naya asked in a worried tone.

"After the service party I'll be heading home to gather up the things I need and start my travels in the morning."

"I see." Naya paused for a moment. "Thank you Ronny.'

"For what? Being here? You know I wouldn't miss it."

"Not that. A General came to my home this morning just as I finished packing. Said I had appoval for an entire year. I don't know what you did in D.C. or have to do for it, but I know you were behind this."

"I plead the fifth." Ronny smiled.

Naya smiled knowing Ronny was never the type to take the credit of most things that he has done in life. To him, it was all about getting things done and making sure the ones that he cared for the most had what they needed. He sacrificed a lot of what he could have for the sake of others and kept the minimal for himself. Even at is age he never slowed down to date and nobody seen much of a married life for him with as much as he worked. Though the service was sad, Naya was happy for all the things that she did have in life.

During the after-party, Naya's two kids Jason and Arial played hide and seek with the other children on base. They were both hiding in the back seat of Ronny's car when Jason noticed a large brown envolope with White House paperwork inside. Curiosity struck him of what secrets it held and he pealed it open slowly to pull out its contents. At first, he thought of it as a Scifi story as he read through the several pages one by one. But he knew what a government report looked like from sneaking peakes at his dad's paperwork whenever he got the chance. Though he loved the Scifi genre, he realized that this was no fatasy book, but a full military report. Knowing what this was, he held the report with one hand and took his sister's hand with the other as he got out of the car.

"Come on." Jason said quickly. "Let's go in the house. I want to make a copy of this for mom."

"Awe, but we are in the middle of a game." Arial pouted as she followed.

"This is important. It's about Ronny's next mission." Jason exclaimed.

"Mommy says you shoulden't snoop through other people's things." Arial points out.

That was all that was able to be said by the time they entered the house and reached the printer/copier. Opening and revealing each page of the stapled report, Jason copied both sides of each sheet. After copying the entire packet, her lead his sister upsteirs and hid the pages under his pillow for later. After the report was hidden away, Jason lead Arial down stairs to replace the origanals in Ronny's car. Once the report was back where it was from, they continued their game with the other children.

Once the party had ended, Naya said her farewells to all the friends and family of the fallen soldier. As she made her way back to the house to clean, she noticed Jason and Arial playing in the back yard. Curious and confused of the sounds that she heard, she went to investigate. They were running around like they normally do when they play, but seemed to be playing on the same side instead of against each other like normal. She made her way across the yard to confront them and their strange game, though she was happy that they we behaving.

"What kind of game are you two playing?" Naya asked, giggling.

"Alien invasion!" Arial replied excitedly.

"You've never played that before. But I'm glad you are getting along."

"Ronny will save us from the aliens that come to extermanate us." Jason chimed in.

"Okay, okay." Naya giggled. "Shoot down a couple of them for me." With that, she walked off towards the house giggling to herself and left them to their game.

Once inside, Naya began to clean what little there was knowing everyone had been decent enough to throw their garbage away. This was one of the things that she had liked the most about living on base when inviting friends over. She was the type to always like her home clean and everyone around her was the same and easy to get along with. Sinece everyone on base were from military families, everything had still been organized and clean other than the dishes. All the kids stayed outside to play to avoid dirty shoeprints and stains on the tile and carpet.

Sighing over the empty house, she grabbed a laundry basket and heded upstairs to the bedrooms to collect clothes. Her first stop was Arial's room knowimg that, other than her own, it was the most organized. Inside the room was spotless and filled with stuffed animals and art projects from drawings to paintings. Just turning six this year, Arial would be starting first grade in the fall, an event in which her father would now miss. Shaking the tearful thought from her mind, she began to collect stuffed animals and ognize them onto the bed by size.

Next, she began to straighten up the tea set on the little table in the middle of the room. On the table near one of the tea cups was a picture of Arial and her dad together on her fifth birthday, just a month before he had shipped out. They had all gone to Bush Gardens for the entire weekend as a final family outing knowing that he would be gone for a year. The picture had been taken on the first day when she had won a stuffed dragon in one of the games. Tears welled up in Naya's eyes as she thought of the remaining days they had spent together as a family.

She placed the picture back onto the table and began to gather up the clothes that we neatly stacked into a pile as she wipped away the tears and thoughts from her mind. Once she had finished, she left and headed across the hall to Jason's messy room. Bracing herself for the mess awaiting her on the other side of the door, she took a deep breath and prepared for the worst. Jason's room was, as she had expected, a mess with plastic army men, dinosaurs, and legos scattered everywhere. Everything was organized in a way, with a paused battle in the middle of the room. The battle had began a week before with legos used for construction, dinosaurs used for secret beast weapons of war, and of corse green army men as soldiers.

Shaking her head with a slight giggle, she turned towards the corner of the room where a small pile of dirty clothes lie in wait. After piling the dirty clothes into the basket, she made her way to the unmade bed to straighten it up. As she made the bed, she noticed the corner of a paper sticking out frm under his pillow. Curious of its contents, she lifted the pillow to reveal a stack of papers that had been copied. She gasped when she noticed the insignia of the White House in the top right-hand corner of thr first page.

It was a military mission statement from the Vice President for Ronny's eyes only. Being the widowed wife of a soldier, she knew the rules of all mission statements. Pure fear ran through her as she lifted the copied packet with shaky hands and a lump in her throat. This had been wrong for him to do and she had to shred it immediately, but stopped whenshe noticed a few strange words. She slowly sat back down and began to read through the statement slowly to understand it.

There had been no way Jason could understand what was in the packet at such a young age. Even she had trouble comprehending every word with her fear and confusion growing stronger. Then, she remembered the game they were playing outside, a game tht they had not played before. This was too convincing to ignore that maybe Jason and Arial coud actually understand what this statement said. Naya had some important calls to make, starting ith Ronny because this was an extremely urgent matter.

CHAPTER 6

The hospital room was small and dim-lit with curtens that covered the windows as the patient slept soundly. A young teen girl had been unconscious fr the past fourteen hours since her crash in the race. A monitor played a steady beat as it read her heartbeat and other vitals as she breathed softly. The young man who drove the GTO during the race the night before sat in a chair on the far wall with his arms crossed and his head down. The teen moaned softly as she began to awake with burry vision and a small headach.

When her vision cme to light, she glanced over to see the man in the chair raise his head and look at her. Realizing who he was and that her face was revealed, her eyes widend but she did no speak. He seemed irritated and concerned at the same time as their eyes met and she looked away. She was not expecting for anyone to see her face, but then she rememberd the accident and looked back toward him. There was no turning back or denying what had happened in the race that had put her in this situation.

"Fifteen." The man said softly. "You are only fifteen with a driver's permit." There eyes had never met each other as he spoke. "Your winnings from the race before is safe with me by the way. I'll keep it until you are released. Your parents and brother are asleep in the waiting room." She sat up in her bed to speak, but he cut her off.

"Don't worry, they don't know anything about the race last night or the ones from the past six months. As far as they know, I accidently cut you off and you crashed. That is what I told them and the police on scen." She looked at him worried and confused, but did not speak.

"No need to worry. You are young and don't need something like this on your record. I have sat down and talked to your family and only have one question for you Mia. With your family history, why do you race?"

Mia cleared her throat and sat in silence as she looked down at her hands and thought of what to say. She knew nothing of him and yet he knew a lot about her, including her name and of her family. The I.V. in her arm iched as she rubbed in and thought about the past six months. She looked up at him and studied the details of his facial and body features as she truly looked at him for the first time. His pitch black hair hung off his sholders and his deep dark eyes pierced hers as he stared back at her and waited patiently for an answer.

He was wairng a thin lether jacket that was unbuttoned and revealed a white tanktop under it. His blue jeans had large holes in the knees and covered the top of his military boots. He looked as if he was a rough guy, but sweet and gental at the same time. She had invated his territory, and yet he saved her life and kept her past a secret from her family and athorities.

"You talked to my family, right?" Mia asked softly. "You know of my family history and what each of them do. My mom the nurse, my dad the NASA engineer, my brother a military mechanic. Now look at me, there is nothing."

"You're a good racer." He replied gleefully.

"I crashed." Mia made a sarcastic laugh.

"I caused that wreck, and I apologize."

"It's okay, maybe raing just isn't for me."

"Don't give up on it just because of one accident. You have done great the last six months for your age. With a little training…" he encouraged.

"Training? From whom? You?"

"Well yeah. After you are out of here. After all, other than your family, everyone knows who you are. What's the point of being known withut being known?" He questioned with half sarcasm.

"I would need a new car if I were to start racing again." She said in hopes of his help.

"And your license, you are not allowed to enter another race until you get them."

"Hey, I was doing just…" Mia started, but was interupted.

"No license, no racing. Or your parents can convince you. Speaking of which, it's their turn to talk to you now that you are awake." With that, he got to his feet and headed towards the door.

"Wait! What's your name?"

"Tristen." Was all he replied with.

The door closed behind him leaving Mia alone with her many thoughts of her future. Flashes of the accident came crashing back as she wondered why she only walked away with a few scraps, bruises and a concussion. All she could remember was the car tipping from the drift and herself blacking out when it landed. The sounds of the door opening jolted her away from her thoughts as her family walked into the room. There eyes were filled with tears as they ran up to the bed in which she lay fully conscious.

"Mia, how are you feeling?" Her mother asked, concerned. "I'm so glad that I was on shift when you came in."

"How are you feeling hun?"

"I'm fine." Mia replied. "Just a bit sore. When can I go home?"

"In a couple of days." Her mother answered. "We need to monitor you gor a bit longer."

"Why were you out so late?" her brother chimmed in. "I didn't even see you leave."

"I....um." mia hesitated. "I can't remember. It was all a blur."

They all watched her as the room grew darker and colder with suspence while waiting for more of a reply. She stared at them all knowing she could not explain what she was doing and why out of shame. Her fother Richard, a long time NASA engineer, who helped develop rockets that sent both satellites and people into space. With the long-term goal of sending people to other planet, such as Mars and beyond, works endlessly on new designs for the perfect ship. His research had won him rewards and the hearts of many with his skilles of rocket science.

His short brown hair was parted neatly to the side and his peering green eyes screamed intelligence. At six feet tall, he stood over most of his family and was the tallest in his line of work. Richard had just descovered a way to program a ship for advanced intersteller travel with people aboard when he recived the call about his daughter. He dropped his work and rushed straight to the hospital without a second thought. Though his research was important to humanity, his family always came first.

Her brother Vance stood at 5'11" and graduated from the career center in auto mechanicsat eighteen. Now at the age of twenty one, he repairs millitary grade vehicles such as jeeps and tanks. He had recently returned home from his tour and visiting with the family for the next few months.

His plans are to help his father with building his next project while he is home with no work. This would be the first project they would be working on together that his father had promised they would do.

Mia's mother Molly, the nurse of the family, stands at 5'5" but is not afraid to rough it up with anyone. Much like her daughter, her long blond hair and blue eyes show much mystery, excitement, and intelligence. After neing a nurse for the past twenty years, she has seen it all from child birth to gunshot wounds. Though she could stomach just about anything, when her own daughter was brought in on a stretcher, her heart sank. She had demanded to be her daughter's nurse and take on the extra hours no matter the cost. After treating her wounds and listening to Tristen's explanation of the crash, she knew there had to be more that he was not saying. When the silence became too unbearable to stand, Mia decided to speak again.

"So…. That guy Tristen. You all talked to him?

"Oh yes!" Molly answered happily. "He seems like a decent and responsible young man from the way he talks. Said he would make sure that his insurance would pay for everything."

"He came in with the ambulance and hasn't left." Harold announced. "He road in the ambulance with you and insisted on staying."

"How long have I been here?" Mia asked.

"About thirteen hours." Molly answered. "It's almost 1:30 in the afternoon and you have been in a coma state since you came in. which is the reason why I would like you to stay for a could more days. Though your injuries were minor, the coma had scared me."

"I understand mom." Mia replied. "But I feel fine. Just a bit confused of what had happend. I am a little sore and hungry though."

"Okay, your father and I will get you something to eat. Anything in paticular that your in the mood for?"

"No, anything is fine."

Both Richard and Molly got to there feet and left the room together leaving Vance alone with his stister. Silance filled the room once again as Vance paced the room and messed with the flowers next to her bed. Mia felt awkward from the silance when she knew that Vance was not the silent type when it came to a family situation. She could see that something was on his mind and it began to scare her of what it might be and what he might say. Her fears came to light when their parents were out of ear shot and she broke the silence herself.

"You havent said much." Mia began. "Is everythig okay?"

"I followed you last night when you left the house." Vance replied.

"You said you didn't see or hear me leave." Mia's eyes widend in shock from his confessed.

"I couldn't let our parents know that you were racing. I watched every race last night and get why you were. I won't take that away."

"So you aren't going to say anything?"

"Not yet I won't. I left just before the race with Tristen so I can think of how to confront you about it. First thing I want to ask is how long have you been racing?"

"About six months ago is when I started. It was just after I got my driver's permit. I snuck out just to go and watch a race and someone challenged me."

"Why didn't you just turn them down?" Vance asked in concern. "And why did you hide your identity?"

"You know I can't turn down a challenge." Mia smiled guilitily. "As for my identity, I wore the suit and helmet on my way there and while I watched the races. I didn't want anyone from my school to see that I went to watch. The rest came with it. After I got the challenge, I raced once and won. That's when everyone labled me 'The Mystery Racer' and it stuck. It was as if I had found my calling like mom and nursing, dad and rocket science, and you with the military."

"There are better and more legal career choices to make than a street racer Mia." Vance scolded gentally.

"Like what? Changing bed pans as a nurse for sixteen hours a day, building rockets for a wopping seventy grand a year, or joining the military as a government lap dog and getting myself killed because others can't get along? No thank you!"

"Is that really what you think of our family? That we became like everyone else and chose a legal career?" Vance asked angerly.

"No, I'm simpally saying that I'm not like you three. I'm different and want to stay different. You may not like it but I love racing and I never want to stop. Since you said that you watched me race, you know that I;m damn good at it as well."

"But you almost gotten yourself killed." Vance changed his tone to that of concern. Before she could reply and defend herself, their parents walked in with food and drinks. She knew that the conversation was far from over and would have to eventually continue the discussion later. For now, they would keep the argument at a pause and spend time as a family while she healed up in the hospital. She knew the life that she wanted and it wasn't what her family wanted from her. Mia did not want to be like them and settle for a normal career with limitations or bounderies. She wanted much much more than a common life with government pay and ideals.

CHAPTER 7

Early summer time in Tampa, Florida had a scorching wet heat and humid air like most of the year in this large state of the south. The sun was high with lunch time aproching as Ronny sat in his car outside the news station waiting for who he was looking for to exit. After his visit in D.C, he knew of one person he could trust with the task he was given by Vice President Aine O'Conner. It had been awhile since he had a visit and knew it was time to make up for it as much as he could. He knew that it had been too long when he saw Naya and her kids and it had made him want too see his own family after what had happened to his best friend.

A young dark-skinned woman of the age of twenty-two made her way out the doors and down the steps. Her short pink hair waved in the breeze as she looked around and spotted Ronny sitting in his car. She wore a short white tank top that revealed her belly button and a black mini skirt that bounced as she made her way to the car with n excited smile from ear to ear. She held her notebook close to her chest with it cupped in both of her arms as she reached the car. Ronny rolled down the window of the passanger side and unlocked the door for her to get in.

"Uncle Ronny!" She cheered as she got in the car. "When did you get back?"

"A few days ago." Ronny answered. "But I had to go to D.C. for a confrence."

"I missed you. It's a great surprise to see you."

"They let you report in that?" Ronny asked when he noticed her clothes.

"Oh hush. I'm grown" She giggled. "And yes, there is no dress code."

"As long as you're happy. How are you doing kiddo?"

"I'm doing great, but I'm not a reporter just yet."

"It's a shame. Your face is made for t.v. and you're good at gathering information."

"I'm working on it uncle." She said with a sigh. "What brings you around so sudden after getting back?"

"I'm working on something important and wanted to talk to you about a few things. Do you have time to grab lunch with me?"

"I always have time for you uncle Ronny. But I was going to be meeting with someone. Could he join us?"

"Sure thing. Where are we going?"

As the car made its way down thr road Ronny's neice Ava explained who they were meeting with. When they arrived at there destination, Ava pointed out a young nerdy guy her age named Aaron. He was a short tan guy with bleach blond hair and blue eyes that came up to Ronny's sholders. His bright hair and eyes shinned in the sun and reflected off his glasses and showed much intelligence. After the interductions, they sat down at and outside dinner table to talk about recent events.

"Congratulations on the engagement you two!" Ronny said pleased with the news. "Do you have a date for the wedding?"

"Not yet." Ava answered. "But we were thinking about sometime next summer."

"Ava wants to get the reporting job that's coming avalible next month before we start planning anything." Aaron joinned in.

"Right." Ava agreed excitedly. "If I can get that job, I can make Aaron my camraman and we would make a great team and income."

"That's amazing you two." Ronny replied. "So, you're a camraman huh? "Ronny thought out loud. "That's interesting."

"Aaron recently graduated from collage with a degree in computer programing and firewall coding." Ava announced proudly.

"You don't say." Ronny rubbed his chin. "maybe I could help you get that reporting job."

"Don't do that uncle Ronny. I don't want to get the job with a military word involved. I want to earn it. I'd feel more accomplished that way."

"I wouldn't dream on interfering like that. But I may have a story that could out you right at the top the the list for that job."

"Really!?" Ava lighted up. "What is it? I need a story like last week. Is it a kick-ass story?"

"You could say that. You help me, I'll help you." Confused and intrigued at the same time, Ava and Aaron looked at each other and then back at Ronny.

"Okay, we're interested." Ava said excitedly. "let us in."

Ronny knotted as his face changed to serious mode as he pulled out his laptop along with a USB drive. Setting them both down on the table, he opened the loptop and plugged in the USB drive. Ava and Aaron watched Ronny quietly as he worked knowing that what he had with him must be something military or government related. As Ava and Aaron moved closer, Ronny opened a window and clicked on the only file within. An auto message began to play and they listened closely as goosebumps covered their bodies with fear.

Once the auto message had ended, Ronny removed it from the laptop and smashed it quietly. After it was destroyed and unusably, he placed it in a to go box on the table and through it away. He them went through the laptop and reset it to factory settings and began to bring up wedding pictures and videos to hide all trace of its past use. Aaron and Ava watched Ronny in shock and disbelief of everything they had just witnessed.

"So, what do you think?" Ronny asked calmly.

"Where did you get this information?" Ava ashed still in shock and a bit of fear in her voice.

"When I was in D.C. for my meeting. It was a very small and secret meeting with the Vice President. Only a few people were there."

"You met the Vice President?" Aaron asked excitedly.

"What is she like?" Ava asked. "She is the youngest in history to get that posistion."

"Well first off she is very stern and powerful minded." Ronny replied. "She also knows what she wants and how to get it. She kind of reminds me of you Ava."

"Oh very funny Uncle." Ava rolled her eyes smiling.

"Did I miss something?" Aaron asked as he looked back and forth between them.

"You'll find out soon enough on your own my boy." Ronny chuckled.

"Anyway." Ava interupted and changed the subject. "Why would you bring this to us? And what could we possibly do to help you?"

Without saying a word, Ronny closed the laptop and placed it back in his bag for later use. Then he turned back to his neice and her future husband as he thought of how to explain everything from the meeting in D.C. He straightened himself up and took in a deep breath as he folded his hands on the table and stared at them both. Ronny cleared his throat and began talking in a low whisper that caught there attention.

"Okay, this is a very long and important story so listen very closely. I can only tell you this once." They both knotted and set their full attention on the deturmend man. "My commanding officer Ayden Vice was taking a trip to D.C. and invited me along for a meeting. When we arrived, we met with Commander Waya Aholoke and Vice President Aine O'Conner. We made our way to a confrence room in the White House and this same message was played to me and the rest of us. When I first heard it, I had the same reaction you did in my mind. Once everyone calmed down, we had to make a plan to tell everyone on Earth of this information. Now there are some people that would want to keep this quiet and save only those who they see fit. The rest of us see that as wrong and want the world to know."

"Only trusted friends and allies can be a part of this plan." Ronny continued. "They needed a reporter for the world announcement so I volunteered you to held. Since Aaron is a cameraman, that kiss two birds with one stone if you accept. If you accept this mission, you will both get to meet Vice President O'Conner and report for her and help announce this message. In turn, this story could also boost your career and get you that reporting job. What do you say to that? Are you two in?"

Excitement, fear, and inerest flowed through Ava and Aaron as they listened to Ronny's mission. They had always dreamed of seeing the White House and meeting the Vice President in person. Reporting for her would be the best thing that they would ever acomplish, but seemed so farfeched before. Weather it was from their career or from a word by Ronny, they wanted to meet Vice President O'Conner and help her release this information to the world. Everyone desurves to know the fate that awaits them so how could they possibly turn this down?

"We're in." Ava announced. "But I have a question. How and where will we be doing this?"

"Vice President O'Conner is, as we speak, setting up a meeting to announce that she will be running for President during the next election."

Ronny replied. "it will be held at the White House and will get the attention of the entire country. And with this kind of announcement, the world would follow and listen in."

"That's a good plan." Aaron said. "But how would the world know? Their goverments would try to cover it up as fake news in some way."

"With your education and skills, we can give you the codes necessary to connect to all stations around the world. This also includes any and all tech that has a screen."

"That's a great cover up and sneaky way to send out the message." Ava started. "But if there are people that want to keep this under wraps, how do we let the world know before they catch on to our plan?" Ronny bent forward and smiled.

"Because the announcement will be carried out tomorrow morning." Ava and Aaron looked at each other then back at Ronny in shock and excitement.

Across the street from the dinner a black car with tinted windows was parked with two men inside. A tall linky man was taking pictures of Ronny, Aaron, and Ava as they talked and finished their meal. A short and round man held a device that listened in on their conversation, but was disapointed in only hearing of wedding plans since they had parked. They had heard that Ronny had just got back from D.C. and went to a funeral, but they had missed the ceremony. Once they had learned he was on his way to meet with someone, they began seasrching for him.

Their tracking had led him to the dinner where he was having lunch with his niece and her future husband. Word had gotten back to them that Ronny was on a mission against the government, but came up short on any evidence. They had decided that it was time to ask him questions and search his things for any physical evidence. Once they had finished their meals, Ronny shook Aaron's hand and hugged Ava before saying their goodbyes. They walked in opposite directions and they watched as Ronny walked to his car on the other block.

The two men decided to head him off and meet him at his car in order to talk in privite. Ronny made his way to the car garage where he had parked and down the ramp to the third level. Once he rounded the corner of level three, he saw two men leaning up against his car next to a large black van. He knew something was about to happen and he braced himself for the outcome. He took a deep breath and walked up to them calmly and smiled as if he had known them.

"May I help you gentalmen?" Ronny asked.

"Yes you can." The pudgy man replied. "Get in the van. We need to have a little chat if you don't mind."

Complying in order to not cause a scene in a public area, Ronny entered the van quietly. the tall linky man followed Ronny's lead and entered the back with him as the pudgy man got into the driver's seat. He quickly obtained Ronny's personal belongings and held them as he started the van. They drove out of the garage and down the block in silence before coninuing their conversation.

"Check his belongings." The round man grumbled as she handed the laptop bag to the quiet man.

Without sayingh a word, the lanky man took the bag with a huff and began searching its contents. All he found inside was a single laptop for personal use that they had seen at the dinner. As he searched through the history and data, he only found pictures and videos of weddings. There was no government data or messages anywhere to be found, nor was there a history before that day of it being used. Fustrated at not finding anything of interest, he placed the laptop back into its bag and shook his head at his parnter to confirm the results.

"I take it that you didn't find whatever it is that you were looking for." Ronny said smugly as he re-aquired his bag.

"I have questions for you>" The pugly guy huffed.

"Shoot. But not literally, I have plans later."

"Those plans are what we need to ask you about. We know you had a small group meeting with Vice President Anie O'Conner recently in D.C. Why?"

"That's all this is about?" Ronny laughed. "Okay, okay, if you want tol know that bad I'll tell you. Vice President Aine O'Conner is announcing tomorrow that she will be running for President come next election time."

"Then what was the purpose of traveling all the way there for that and then back here just to go back tomorrow?" the Pugly man snarled.

"My niece is trying to get a reporting job and is getting married next year. I wanted to see the man she will marry so we had lunch. And I thought that reporting for the Vice President's announcement would garrentee her the reporting job. The job is coming avalible next month and she needs a 'kick-ass story' as she would say. I thought I would giver her the chance. You don't do much research do you big fella?"

Feeling stupid and embarrassed about not knowing information of his family before acting, the chubby man fell silent. Not wanting to reveal what they were looking for, just in case he really knew nothing, the round man thought carefully about what to say next. Considering that this was a life or death situation, he had to be very careful of everything he did or said to Ronny. If he knew something and was let go, they would be the ones to pay for failing the mission. But if he knew nothing and was kill for no reason, things would take a turn for the worst with the death of an innocent soldier.

"Was this the only reson for the visit with your niece?" The pudgy man asked.

"Well no." Ronny replied. "Not only was she engaged and needed a report, but I haven't seen her in quite awhile because I was overseas fighting. I wanted to make up for lost time. Plus im back her because I just went to my friend's funeral as well."

"I see." The round man scrached his chin.

"What are you looking for exactly? I am quite confused. Did something happen that I should know about?"

"No… we're sorry for the inconvenience."

The van drove around the block and back into the garage and parked next to Ronny's car. The ride back was silent and awkward with no more questions that they could ask Ronny without saying too much. Once they let Ronny out of the van, they apologized again for the trouble and left it at that. They had to do a lot more research on Ronny before they could confront him again. But in the mean time, they would have to keep a close eye on him just in case they missed something. After the van drove away out of sight, Ronny got into his car and smiled brightly after making them look like idiots.

CHAPTER 8

The flight from Tampa to D.C. was long and stressful for Ronny, Ava, and Aaron as they mentally prepared themselves for the events to come. A large secret service limo met them at the airport ready to take them to the White House to meet with Vice President O'Conner. Aaron was preparing his laptop for the codes to connect to the multiple networks around the world. Ava was silently practicing her speech to introduce Vice President Aine O'Conner, in which she spent half the night preparing. Ronny was quietly watching the scenery pass by as he thought of how big today was for them and the entire world.

As they approched the White House, shivers of fear, excitement, and reality flooded all three of them with the tasks that were about to take place. The entire world was about to learn of a great and myserious truth that mankind has been asking for centeries. Approching the front gates, the limo came to a stop in front of two armed guard as they stood at attention. Ronny could not beleave his eyes when he seen that it was the same two men that had taken him for a ride back in Tampa the day before. The first thought that flooded his mind was that they were hired by Aine to see if he was trustworthy enough with the task at hand.

"It's good to see you again Mr. Davis." The short pudgy man said with a smile.

"Likewise." Ronny replied.

Ava and Aaron could feel the tention between the two men and chose to keep to themselves and their work. Once they were all out of the limo, they followed the two men to the front doors of the White House. Ava and Aaron were mesmerized by the massive interior of the historic building. There were pictures on every wall and large white stone pillers that connected the floor with the celling. In the middle of the room was a lage carpet with the Presidental seal printed upon it.

The small group was guided up the winding staircase to the secend floor and were the meeting room was located. Once they reached the second floor, they turned left down the hallway to the fourth door. Ronny reconized it as the same door that he had met with Vice President Aine O'Conner the morning before. When they enterd the room, they were met by Aine O'Conner, Ayden Vice, and Waya Aholoke. They were all sitting around the table waiting for their arrival to the pre-announcement meeting.

"Oh great, you're here." Aine said pleased. "You two can help the rest of secirity set up the podium and get everything ready." She told the two secret sevicemen. "I announce my running in an hour and I want everything to be perfect." They bothe nodded and closed the door behind them. Once they were out of earshot, the conversation continued from where it left off.

"Were you the one that sent dumb and dumber to watch and test me Aine?" Ronny asked.

"Not those two." Aine explained. "When I found out that others had known about the message, I sent someone to see if you were safe. Then I called secret service and had those two hired as security."

"Why would you hire people who would be a threat to your mission?" Ava asked.

"It's a keep your friends close but your enemies closer tactic." Aaron replied.

"That's right." Aine confirmed. "Having them here where we can watch them is better than them being able to use spyware on us."

"Fair enough." Ronny said. "How many people do we have to cover us if things go bad?"

"Everyone in this room is all we have and need for the task at hand." Waya chimed in. "You, Ayden, and I will keep an eye on our new security during the announcement."

"Right." Ayden agreed. "All while Aaron and Ava do their job reporting the message as the reporting team."

"The rest of the security and White House staff comes with my job and has clearence through the government." Aine began. "Aaron, these are the codes you will need to tap into every station and screen around the globe. You have less than a half hour to get them ready. But don't broadcast until just before Ava introduces me."

"Right." Aaron replied. "I will get started and meet you all outside."

Massive crowds of people were gathered around the live meeting podium outside the gates of the White House. Eager faces of Aine O'Conner's fans awaited her last minute presidental announcement. Every news station truck was lined up on both sides of the street outside a perimeter that was blocked off by police. Reporters from every news station checked themselves and their camera crews as they prepared for the announcement that was about to be underway. Ava and Aaron were a part of this crowd of reporters as they set up closer to the podium with White House clearence IDs.

With nobody daring to get in their way, they had free range to set up their camera and prepare to introduce the Vice President. After entering his coding, Aaron nodded to Ronny, who in turn nodded back to confim. He then set up his camera to view the podium in the background and plugged a cord from his laptop to the camera. Ava stood in front of the camera and checked herself for the most important report of her life. Aaron activated the the camera and sent the feed to every screen in the world as Aine took a deep breath for her appearance.

"In five, four, three, two." Aaron couted down and pointed to Ava.

"Greetings to you all." Ava began. "We are live here in Washington D.C. My name is Ava Statin and I am standing here outsided the White House awaiting Vice President Aine O'Conner's important announcement." With hearing her introduction, Aine braced herself and casually walked out to the podium waving. All eyes and cameras from around the world were on her as she took a deep breath and spoke.

"Good morning to everyone and thank you very much for coming to this meeting on such short notice. To satisfy your curiosity of the rumors that are going around, yes I am running for president during the next election. I will be taking questions about this at the end, but first there is a much more important announcement to make at the moment." As

Aine continued her speech, she pulled out her laptop and a USB drive. Without hesitation of the consiquences that may happen, she plugged in the USB drive and pulled up an autio message link. "A NASA worker picked this up from a satellite less than 72 hours ago and I have made it my mission to reveal it to the world no matter the cost. There are those who wish to keep this under wraps, but I refuse to be a figure head like a lot of government officials. The world desurves to know of its fate and I will be the one to let them know even if I die today." Aine took a deep breath before pressing play.

At that moment, Penguin and Lester, the two secret service agents, realized what was about to unfold in front of the world and quickly acted. Lifting the Glock-nines from their hosters at their sides, they took aim at Aine without a second thought. But before they could pull their triggers, they were met by Ayden and Ronny as they pointed their nine-millimeters between their eyes. Knowing that they couldent call for backup while in the line of fire, the two agents dropped their weapons and waited for their people to act. They fell to their knees and held their hands up high to surrender knowing it was their only way to live.

As the speaker volume was turned up, a sniper leaned out of the window on the top floor of a ten-story building. With the distance of three hundred yards away, the sniper locked onto Aine's head ant prepared to fire his one and only shot. The door burst open from behind him and he was met by Waya Aholoke and three soldiers hired by Ayden. Before any of them could make a move, the autio message began to play for the world to hear. Aaron locked the codes in and every screen in the world was locked onto Aine O'Conner with no way to turn them off.

A deep and scratchy voice with a German accent came over the speakers as the message began to play:

"Greeting to all the human race from beyond the starts. Our people have researched your satellite feed for quite a few years now and learned much of your species. We have decided to come to Earth for a visit with our own intentions. But not one of you shall be happy with these intentions we have in mind. Your planet's atmosphere and resources are perfect to sustain life for many years in your galaxy. But I'm afraid that your species is questioned. You rage war amongst yourselves for the most pettiest reasons. These reasons include race, religion, greed, cultural differences, and land. You are nothing more than lost beasts in the fight for survival. Your pittiful race is nothing more than an eye sore and an abomination to nature. For this, you should not be allowed to exsist within this universe. Therefore, our species has decided to pay a visit to youe planet and exterminate your filth and sell your planet to a worthy species. Due to our long list of places to be, we don't have the time to make our way there now, so this message is enough to help you prepare for your finnal days of life. We shall arrive at your planet in approximentely three years from now. Your civilization is not advanced enough to fight back, nor is it capible of gaining such technology to do so with you devided personalities. With that being said, there is no fear in telling you this. Farewell Earth! And enjoy your last three years of existence! AHAHAHAHA!"

Once the message had ended, the entire world was silent with pure fear and anger. The two servicemen fell to their knees in shame for what they had tried to stop the world from hearing. They had no idea of what the message was truly about and would gladly take any punishment that came their way. Those who are in charge only let it be known that there was a government related message that needed to be kept secret no matter the cost. The orders were clear to stop it from being revealed no matter the extreme that had to be taken.

All across the world people developed different emotions as Aine O'Conner reapeared on the screen. Every eye was piericed on their t.v.'s waiting for the answers of the terrifying message. Mia and her family watched intenslly as Aine closed her laptop with seeccess and raised her eyes to the camera. Mia sat up in her hospital bed with her hand over her mouth and tears in her eyes as Tristen gave her a comforting hug. He of all people knew that he would soon be called to arms and have to perpare for the biggest fight of his life.

On the other side if the country Naya held Jason and Arial close to her on the couch as they watched the horror of Ronny's paperwork come to light. They knew he would be called to arms and that he put them in the saftey of the military base for this reason. She slowly grabbed her phone to call family but the cell rang as she looked at the screen. Her sister was calling and she felt that she read her mind because that was the first call on Naya's list. Life as they knew it was about to change, though they didn't know if it was for the better or worse.

"I know everyone is in shock." Aine began. "I was in in shock as well when I first heard it. Just like you, it was and still is hard to beleave. But this is very real and we only have three years to act on this. Yes I am running for president during the next election and will put all my efforts into a plan that will save us all. Ever since I was given this message, I have been working around the clock building a team to relay this to the world. I am very sad to inform you all that there are those who tried to hide this information from the world. Most of them are the world leaders and sadly includes our very own President who has tried to assainate me and my small team. Because of this situation, my plan is very simple yet hard to accomplish because of our differences.

The alien species is right that we are devided and that is why I say that it is time to tear down that wall and rebuild together. From this day forward, I hear by recommend that we dismiss any and all feuding in all countries in order to survive this future invasion. The last 72 hours my team and I have came to only one alternitive in surviving this attack. We could put all of our time, effert, and resources into building an Arc System of ten ships with experimental tech we have been past ready to try. This can be accomplished as long as we work together as one world instead of devided countries.

For now, it is best if we left Earth behind until we know that we can win and gain everything back. I know it is a lot to ask, but this may be our only chance to survive as a species and live to fight another day. With this new evidence of intelligent life, there could also be good species out there that may be able to help. Just like every war, we need allies to win and protect what we hold dear to our hearts. We only have one chance and your decision alone will decide weather we live or die and how we choose our own fate, as everyone should. The choice is yours! Please, I beg you all, listen to my words and choose with your hearts."

An uproar began in the crowd of fear, anger, and questions as Aine tried to retake control of the meeting. She decided to remain silent until everyone calmed down, though it seemed like hours. When she would not budge on answering questions or fighting back, everyone subsided and awaited for the next part of her speech. The crowd watched and waited in antisipation as Aine took a deep breath and continued where she left off.

"I know this will anger a lot of you, including certin groups who dislike certin types of people." Aine began and her voice became stern and angry with seriousness of the situation. "But we do not have the time for petty differences amongst ourselves. It is time for us to stop behaving like children and bullying each other for such stupid things like the voice said in the message. If we could have changed a long time ago, maybe we wouldn't be in this situation, or at least be able to fight back without having to abandon our homes. We are all at fault and should recognize this in order to grow bigger as a species. It has been proven that when we put our minds together, we can accomplish what was said to be impossible. It is time to do just that and prove that we desurve to live.

We do not have the time or technology to fight and win an intergalactic war currently. But we do have the time and resources to build these Arcs in order to escape our fate of exstinction and live to fight when we obtain that together. Devided we will most certinlly fall. But together we shall survive."

Once again, the crowd roard, not with angery questions this time, but with calm voices and concerned questions. Again, Aine remained silent for the crowd to calm down and await her answers and plans. She knew that in this situation, it was natural for people to uproar with anger, concern, and multiple questions. But she also knew that patience was key to getting the point across and calming people down by letting them get the anger out. Yet again, the crowd ended their questioning and calmed down for Aine to continue her speech.

"After coming to a global compromise, the next thing we must do is begin deconstructing every town and city in the world to use those resources to build the Arcs. We will be housed as if in the middle of a war with medical and housing tents with world wide military support. This will be a full three year prosses and we need every availible man and woman in order to succeed. After that, we will have all construction worker personel along with NASA working together all around the world to start building the greatest ships we have ever created. During that time, the rest of the world will be farming and gathering all plant and animal species so they will not be caught in the exstintion. Plus we will need them in order to survive our journey through the stars. The project will start within a week or two depending on the people of the world and their actions."

When Aine finished her speech and let herself calm down from her own rage of the upcoming events, the crowd flooded with questions of the future. As she answered each question, everyone in the world was glued to their t.t's or ourside screens depending on their locations. While watching the breaking news update, people all around the world were on their phones with family and friend planning their next move. They all knew that the next or possibally the last three years of their lives would be the busiest and most stressful time they ever had.

CHAPTER 9

Three months had past since the day Aine O'Conner revealed the terrifying message to the world. But for the first month, the world was in full chaos with riots and eople who were scared to death from the reality. Many suicides flooded the world with fear of not being able to get along and die in the ands of invaders. Waya and Aine did what they could to calm the people down with daily confrences and global announcements. Ronny and Ayden traveled non-stop to lead rallies of peace and help to every citizen of Earth.

Once they finally got control of everyone and they calmed down, the deconstruction project began. The world government came together and arrested those who were involved in trying to stop the intergalatic message from being revealed to the people. Aine O'Conner was voted into office as the new offical President for her courageous fight to help the world. But she wasn't just the President of the USA, the world government had made her the President of human kind. She had accepted in order to lead the human race to safty and succeed in escaping the war they knew they couldn't win.

Now with everyone working together as one, the world deconstruction project is nearing its end. The prosses of clearing out the building sites of the ten Arcs had began just a few days prior. Though nature has taken a toll of this development, the entire country of Canada had been flattened out in ten Texas sized sites. 7.5 billion people began making their way from all around the world to build the greatest ship they had ever created. Each Arc would be the size of three New York Cities and each Arc Station would host ten persent of the human race to board each Arc.

Richard Price, husband of Molly and father of Vance and Mia, stood at the future site of Acr One with his IPod in hand. At the edge of site one stands a tower that will connect to Arc One and hold it in place as it gets built. Scrolling through the blueprints, Ritchard makes his final touches of the arc when he was met by a small group of officals. Aine O'Conner, Waya Aholoke, Ayden Vice and Ronny Davis locked eyes with one another and nodded when they reached Ritchard. He tucked his IPod under his arm and smiled as he shook hands with each of the world saviors.

"It's an honor to finally meet you in person Mr. Price." Aine said pleased.

"The pleasure is all mine Madam President." Richard replied. "It was a shame that the former President was behind your assasination attempt and had to be taken down with the rest. I know how much you looked up to him."

"It's alright. In the end, he never wanted this released to the people and put the entire world at risk. Anyway, that was the past and we must look to our future. This is Commander Waya Aholoke, Commander Ayden Vice, and Captain Ronny Davis."

"It's an honor to meet all of you. You are right that we should look to the future, and this Arc shall be our greatest achievement. My son Vance is a military mechanic, my wife Molly is a nurse, and my daughter Mia is a softmore in high school." Ritchard introdused his family. "They are standing over by the Arc site right now. My daughter has yet to find a place in life, but she is still young."

"She will in time." Ronny pitched in. "My niece was the same way until about a month before she graduated high school. Now she is a reporter."

Being the strong silnt type, Ayden remaind quiet while they talked as he noticed the semi trucks pull up to site one with materials. Ayden signaled the others of the arrival of the workers to their most important job and they began walking to greet them. Thousands of workers began to surround the building site as the semis dropped off hundreds of tons of materials that will be used for the skeletal outline of Arc One. Several tractors, forklifts, and many other machins began to pick up materials and drive to their desiganted spots.

The workers hauled beam after beam and stood them in lines around the base of the building site. On the inside of the beam perimitor, the workers lay iron platforms and began welding the main external belly. Cranes lifted beams onto one another as they touched the sky and welders began fusing each one together until they reached two hundred stories high. Each section was welded to the next in line severl miles away until the skeleton was fully formed. The world leading group watched in amazment as their greatest creation came to life.

It took several days and nights of non-stop work from several shifts of workers to create the massive outline of the greatest ship humans had ever created. Ritchard spent most of his time traveling between the ten Arc sits scanning the progress and talking to each of the leading teams. Every tean worked fourteen hour shifts seven days a week for three weeks befor the full skeletal form of each Arc was complete. Aine O'Conner lead groups to every site checking on the progress daily as she sent out her reports to all who wasn't working on the Arcs. She met with Ritchard as he was checking on Arc Ten close to the shores north east of Niagra Falls.

"I heard that all ten Arcs were ready for the next step of preperation." Aine began. "I thought I'd come hear it straight from the horses mouth."

"You would be correct." Richard replied with a small laugh. "We are ready to start the next phase of building on your command Ms. President. The trucks have arrived yesterday with everything we need to build the outer shell of each ship."

"In that case, I think everyone desurves a day off for all tgheir hard work. Plus we should be a bit ahead of scedual and I would like to make an announcement and update everyone."

"I'll tell my workers the plans. My son Vance is with Tristen doing the final checks."

"Good to hear. What are the accident and death tolls during the construction?"

"Twelve serious but non-permanent injuries, thirty-two minor injuries, and one fatality."

"That is better than expected. Just take it easy and try to lower that numer the best you can. I'll get preperations ready for my announcement and get back with you."

⸻◆◆◆⸻

Vance was walking with Tristen through the construction site as everyone was taking a lunch break. They had been named the leading formen of the Arc System Project since day one and have been helping every team stay on scedual and stay as safe as possible. They had their own lunches in hand and ready for a rest when they saw Richard approching them. They knew from the look on his face that it had been a good day and that he also had good news. Richard had reached them just as they sat down to eat and he signaled that they wouldn't have to get up.

"How are things going today boys?" Richard asked.

"Just fine dad." Vance replied. "I take it that you have good news for us."

"I do. Actually since the base of the Arcs are complete, Aine has given everyone the day off from working and wants to make a world announcement."

"that's great." Tristen replied." "We have been working like dogs and could use a break. After all, the hard part hasn't even started yet. After we complete the external shell of the ships, we will start on the internal. That will be by far the hardest part. We could probably use a break in between each section. Our men are exhusted."

"I agree with you and will pass it on to Aine when she sends me her update. Let your groups know while I make my rounds to the other Arcs to spread the news."

"No problem dad." Vance said. "The will be exstatic about finally getting a break." They nodded to each other and Richared began to walk away but Tristen stopped him.

"Mr. Price? Could I talk to you about Mia please?"

A day off was announced throughout the ten Arc sites as Aine began her preperations for her world meeting. Aaron and Ava began to set up their equiptment for the meeting happening within the next few hours. Ever since the world announcement of their fate, they had been the personal reporters for Aine and Waya. While they finished their jobs, Waya was preping the security, though none was needed since the feuds had been dismissed for the past two and a half months of construction. Within the hour, everything was ready to go as the crowds began to arrive.

"In three, two, one." Aaron said as her pointed to Ava in front of the camera.

"Good morning to all on this Fine day." Ava began. "Though it is the last day of summer and fall is about to begin, so is a major project. Behind me President Aine O'Conner is about to make an announcement of our progress on the Arc System." Aaron pointed the Camera to the Podium as Aine stepped up to the mic.

"Good morning everyone." Aine says happily. "I an pleased to inform all of you that we are making exillent progress on the Arc System project. For this, I feel that you all desurve an entire weekend off to spend some time with your families." With the changed timeline, the crowd burst with excitement. "We do not want anyone falling over from exhustion so I think that it is best that we have these breaks in between each completed section of the Arcs. We have had several injuries, some minor some bad, and one death so far. This I am sad to report and my heart goes out to the family of the one fatality.

We have all been putting our blood, sweat, and tears into these Arcs and for that I thank you all. As many of you have heard, I am getting married soon and I expect to keep these plans. So it's only fair that all of you get the same kind of time to have a life even through these hard times. Make your plans and I will pass them through and let you take your life plans to their end. Children still go to school and we have graduations every summer as planned. Weddings and funerals still go on and will not be postponed."

The crowd roard with praise and excitement for the unexpected announcement for time off for life plans. It had been such a stressfull three months that nobody expected to have a break until the project was fully complete. With less than three years left before they leave Earth, it was great to hear that they still get to enjoy the time they had left on the planet they called home. The entire world has done more for each other during the past few months than they have their entire lives. They had all realized that world piece had come to pass and they had the weekend to celebrate the historical event.

"Though we still have quite a bit to do in the next couple years," Aine continued. "We are slightly ahead of scedual and have accomplished more than expected. On top of that, we have all come together as one and accomplished the most important thing, we accomplished piece amongst humanity. I am so proud of all of you and I am glad to have the honor in leading humanity as one instead of devided. Now most of this everyone anlready knew and this isn't the only reason I set up this meeting. I have exciting news that will soon help us as a spcies and accomplish our goals of life much sooner than expected.

During the past month, our satellite experts have been working around the clock trying to find us a new home using the same radio waves that sent us that horrifying message. I am pleased to inform you that it was a success and we have found a suitable place for us to call home. I will let the one who discovered this information explain the details. I introduce Aaron McKlain."

Aaron nervosly made his way to the podium where Aine stood and shook his hand. Ava directed the camera as Aaron pulled out his laptop and plugged in his USB drive. The white screen behind him lit up with the screen from the laptop for the world to see. He took a deep breath as he launched the programshowing a #d animation of the universe.

"The radio signal led us to a place called the Milky Way Grand Syatem." Aaron began. "As you all know, NASA has picked up thousands of radio signals from beyond our solar system for years. Though we couldn't truly find their locations, but with the message we recived we were able to trace it back to other systems. We believe this is a 'man made' solar system so to speak. The entire system gives off many signals but shows no sign of a natural sun and is in the location of our galaxy that we believed to be just dead space. Many different languages were deciphered giving us a reason to believe that there are several species living together in peace. This is good news and we are working around the clock to get in contact with them and maybe even get help."

Thousands of questions flooded the crowd with this new information and Aine with concerns and Aine and Aaron did their best to answer them all. Due to the worldwide deconstruction project, everyone now lived in military tent and had very little room from them all being side by side in rows. The only thing that remained from the old life of humanity was the large television screens served for only news and announcements. Entertainment productions were put on hold until further notice as they all did their part to help any way that they could. Every piece of land in the world, other than the country of Canada that was used for the Arc

System, was being used to farm for food and supplies so that everyone can survive their journey into the great beyond.

After the announcement, Aine made her way to her tent and sat down at her desk in her office. Laying her head down on her desk, she closed her eyes and rested a moment from her long day and even longer three months. But her comercial nap din't last long once there was a knock on her door and Waya walked in. Feeling guilty from seeing her in such a miserable state, he slowly crept up to her desk and tapped her shoulder. She slowly lifted her head and their eyes locked as he saw the bags under her eyes and he frowned.

"It's okay Waya." Aine said as she straitened up in her chair. "What is it that you need?"

"What I need is for you to get some sleep." Waya replied as he put a lot of emphasis on the 'I'. :But the council needs some papers signed for the next phase of building."

"Signed and stamped before I even sat down." She pointed to a stack of papers next to her laptop. "Also, sleep is for the dead, and I'm very much alive."

"I can see this." Waya chuckled. "But you tell everyone else to take a few days off and you don't. maybe you should take your own advice."

"Don't lecture me!" she snapped with a playful glare knowing he was right.

"Come on, up." Waya chuckled again. "I have a jeep waiting for us outside."

"Where are we going? And what about the paperwork that you interupted my nap for? Which you tried to scold me for by the way."

"I only do because I care. And you will see when we get to where we are going. As for the paperwork, I'll let them know it's on your desk." Without another word, Aine nodded and let Waya help her to the jeep for his surprise trip.

CHAPTER 10

Ten full months had past since the Earth had received the terrifying invation message that sent them into chaos and forced humanity to make decisions they normally wouldn't. thirty percent of exterior of each Arc has been complete and anouther break was announced for two special occasions. Two weddings are scedualled for the weekend for Aine and Waya on a live report along with Ava and Aaron the next day. Preperations were being prepared as Aaron set up his camera and Ava took down notes from the in peron guests as they arrived. Under a large white tent family and close friends of Aine and Waya sat and awaited the ceremony to begin.

Ronny, naya and her kids sat in the second row along with the Price family across the aisle from them. The rest included the former world leaders who had stepped down for Aine when the Arc project began. In the left-hand corner of the tent sat a white haired man playing the piano as the priest and Waya awaited Aine's appearance. Beyond the tent doorway, Aine stood and took a deep breath then stepped forward through the tent flaps. She slowly crept down the red carpet in the senter of the aisle as everyone watched her every move.

Her long white dress fluttered as she walked and her vail covered her face and her nervous smile. Holding a bauquet of white roses hin her hand, she walked u to the podium whhere the priest stood and joined Waya's side. The man behind the piano played the final verse and stopped to indicate that the wedding ceremony was about to begin. The priest cleared his throat and smile at Aine and Waya as he opened the bible to a spot marked by a cross.

"Good morning to all of you." The priest began. "Thank you all for coming to this very special event. Today we unite Aine O'Conner ans Waya Aholoke as one in holy matrimony. Today they shall be wed and begin their lives together with love and start a family. This is a day of love and peace and should be celebrated as such. If there is anyone who believes that these two should not be wed, please speak now or forever hold your peace." The crowd sat in silence and smiled brightly. "In that case, you may now exchange your vows."

"Aine my love." Waya began. When we first met, I thought that you were just another politician that I was hired to guard. You were very distant with even the most basic talk and very into your work. But after you began to open up, I realized how much we had in common with how things should be. You cared more for the voice of the people than the people that you worked for. You refused to be a figurehead and controled from behind the scenes. My dream was to unite the world and I realized that yours was the same. I quickly fell in love with everything you stood for and everything you wanted to be. Know that even if the universe is against you that I'll always be here by your side supporting you one hundred persent of the time. There is no other person in the universe that I'd rather spend my life with than you."

"Waya my love." Aine began. "when we first met, I though of you as just another jarhead looking for a paycheck. You were silent most of the time and stuck to your mission like any other soldiar. We didn't get along at first because of your stubborness and my work. But your stubborness made me determinded to open you up and I began to talk about myself. When I finally got you to open up, I realized just how passionate you were about the world and what you wanted from it. Though you had every reason to, you never held a grudge against anyone. Among every person in the world, your people were wronged the most by the same government that you worked for. Instead of having hate, you tried to use what you learned to better the world. I fell in love not only with the way you felt about your work, but also the way you treated people. I will alsways follow the path you walk, no matter the cost."

Once they had finished exchanging their vows, there was a moment of silence in the tent. Aine's eyes were filled with tears of joy as they held hands and stood face to face with one another. Waya stared into Aine's eyes and smiled as he thought of the life they were about to spend together. Ending the silence, the priest gently closed the bible and cleared his throat once again. The anticipation of the final speech was just as intense for the crowd as it was for both Aine and Waya as the stood in wait.

"Do you Waya, take Aine to be lawfully wedded wife to have and to hold through sickness and in health till death do you part?" the priest asked.

"I do." Waya said without hesitation.

"Do you Aine, take Waya as your lawfully wedded husband to have and to hold through sickness and in health till death do you part?" the Priest asked again.

"I do." Aine answered happily.

"Then by the power invested in me by the planet Earth, I now pronounce you husband and wife. You may now kiss."

Waya held Aine's chin as he kissed her lips deeply while the crowd cheered for their new lif together. Ava and Aaron stood and clapped as they thought about their own wedded being held the next day. Waya picked Aine up and headed out of the tent with her and began walking to the next tent for their afterparty. Everyone followed suit as the world watched in awe as their new leaders broke bounderies and brought everyone together.

<hr />

Waya and Aine stood together as they both held their knife and cut the wedding cake while everyone cheered. The guests sat at their tables and ate food as they talked about life and their futures and the progress of their new homes being built. Music played while others danced and celebrated the occasion and put their fears on hold for the day. Ava and Aaron talked about their wedding for the next day and made last minute decisions. Ronny walked up to Naya while she watched Jason and Arial dance with the other children.

"Reminds me of your wedding just over a decade ago." Ronny announced as he reached Naya.

"Don't remind me." Naya said, covering her face in embarrisment. "You got drunk and tripped over a chair. You almost broke your neck."

"But I didn't. and you know I was the life of the party. Besides, my best friend had just got married and I was alone at the time."

"Awe poor baby. Go out on a date instead of just flirting with random girls. Besides, there is no deployment anymore. You have a chance to start a life and maybe have kids of your own."

"You're right I guess. I do have my eye on a couple girls."

"Poor things. They better run while they have a chance." Naya giggled.

"Haha funny! You're not so great to be around sometimes either brute. Anyway, you think you will ever date again?"

"I don't know." Naya sighed. "If I do, it will be a few years."

"Take your time and focus on the kids until you figure things out. Besides, it's going to be busy the next few years."

The party soon came to an end as the guests began to leave and spend the rest of the weekend with family. Others stayed behind and helped clean up and prepare for Ava and Aaron's wedding the next day. Waya and Aine headed to their tent and decided to stay behind to see the next wedding before going on their honeymoon. Aaron suddenly heared a beeping sound coming from his tent and went to investigate any updates. When Ava reached the tent, she cpvered her mouth when she saw Aaron bring up something strange on his laptop and they both ran to Aine and Waya's tent.

Mia and Tristen lay under the stars as they held each other and thought about the day's events. They had been dating for the past seven months though they haven't had much time to spend together. Mia was busy with school and Tristen was busy helping with the Arc construction project. Once a week they try to spend an hour or two together other than the weekends that they get to visit one another when breaks are announced. After seeing the wedding that day, they thought about their own lives after Mia would graduate in the next two years.

"Makes you wonder how many of those stars light up a world like ours." Tristen said as he stared up at the night sky. "my wish and dream is to race among them and enter the greatest race the galaxy has to offer."

"That would be a great dream to follow." Mia began. "But you will always be second best to me." She said sarcasticly as she rolled her eyes.

"Why do you say that? You only raced me once you know."

"Yeah and I almost won that race until you tried to kill me." She glared playfully.

"Haha funny that you think you could beat me. And I would never kill a rival, or a girlfriend."

Mia leaned in and kissed him on the lips. "That's all you get until I graduate."

"What a ball buster. Is this because I told you no racing until you got your license?" but she only replied with a giggle and another kiss.

The long relaxing night moved on as everyone slept off the excitement of the day. Sunlight began to shine over the horizen and brought about a new day and another wedding. But not everyone was making preperations for joining in on Ava and Aaron's day of celebration. Waya and Aine were making preperations for an announcement to the world from what the wedding couple had brought to them the night before. Though it was a weekend for a well desurved break, there was work to be done before the week was over.

"Then it's settled," Waya began. "We will make the announcement after the reception party this afternoon."

"I know it's sudden, but the world does need to know what we had found." Aine answered. "Once the construction project continues, we will deal with this new information."

"Do you want Ava and Aaron to report for you on this?"

"No, they desurve their day. Besides, after we make our announcement, we will take our honeymoon as well and then work on this with them when we are all back."

"Well, then we should get ready. The wedding starts in an hour."

Aaron and Ava's wedding began as planned with Waya and Aine watching in the second row with other family and friends. Just like the wedding the day before, they exchanged their vows and nobody interupted them. Ronny had given Ava away and was happy and sad at the same time to see her go. Once they had finished their vows, the priest took his que and slowly closed the bible and cleared his throut. With only one thing left to do, the crowd watch in antisipation for the conclusion of the special event.

"Do you Aaron, take Ava to be your lawfully wedded wife to have and to hold through sickness and in health till death do you part?" The priest asked.

"I do." Aaron answered with a smile.

"Do you Ava, take Aaron to be your lawfully wedded husband to have and to hold through sickness and in health till death do you part?"

"I definitely do." Ava replied happily.

"Then by the power invested in me by the planet Earth, I now pronounce you husband and wife. You may now kiss."

The crowd roard with excitement and joy as the young newlyweds kissed passionately and finallized their life long partnership. Just as the last wedding, everyone made their way to the next tent for the reception party. The guests danced and ate food while the reporters outside prepared for the speech being held after the reception. Though it was a happy moment, Ava could tell that there was a lot on Aaron's mind from the night before. What they had found on his laptop would change everything for the human race and would be revealed within the next couple hours.

"I know it's our wedding day," Ava began. "But what's on your mind? Is it about our discovery last night?"

"Not just that." Aaron replid. "It's also the state of the world. We only came together because we were backed into a corner from the threat of extermanation. It shouldn't be that way."

"It is how we met after all. Remember our second year in collage and I was in creative writing and you had your comuter programing. You were so scared when I asked you for a favor."

"I wasn't scared! Just cautious."

"I'd believe that if I wasn't the only girl you have ever dated in your life." Ava giggled.

"No fair! Besides, you needed my camera for a project."

"Yes, but aren't you glad that you agreed?"

"More than you'll ever know" Aaron kissed her once more.

The reception slowly came to an end as the guests began leave the tent and saw camera crews outside. Baffled by what they saw, questions flooded the area as everyone gathered around. Ava and Aaron knew what was going on and went to their tent to change for Aine's announcement. Though they weren't reporting, they wanted to be comfortable for the event to come. Anie and Waya stepped up to the podium just as the cameras signalled every screen worldwide once more.

"Good afternoon to you all." Aine began. "I am sorry for the inconvenience of this announcement, but our NASA staff had made a discovery last night and was brought to my attention. The world needs to know where it stands and what we have to look forward to in the future. Ronny Davis and Ritchard Price will disscuss what was found and we will all take questions at the end. First you will hear from Richard Price."

"Thank you Mrs. President." Richard replied as he stepped up to the podium. "First I want to say that our team at NASA have been working around the clock looking for a new home for us all. Though there are many planets that could host us that are simular to Earth, finding a way there is hard. Building these Arcs are the only way we would be safe enough to make it to such a detination. But last nigh, we found a radio signal from a sace that we believed to be just dead space. A place with no starlight or planets. I pure black spot in the galaxy with no signs of life. It turns out that we were wrong. There is an entire system there that has multiple signals showing signs that thousands of species living together in peace. We know this because we used the same radio signal that sent use the threat of extinction. At this moment, we are trying to get in contact with them and see if they have room for us. I will update more as we make discoveries. For now, Ronny will take it from here."

"Okay, do I'm not the speech type." Ronny began. "This is my first time in this situation so bare with me. At this time I lead an army of new recrutes that will be talking to whatever amy we get in contact with in the radio singal area. My job is simple yet hard to do. It is to keep us safe and make sure those who we contact are not hostal, but helpful to us. The system we have found is larger than our own solar system and is the best chance we have to survive as a species. For now, that is all I have to say. Our President will answer any and all questions that can be answered at this time."

After all questions were asked, the four newlyweds packed up their things and got themselves ready for their honymoons. Two privet jets awaited their arrival as all the guests said their goodbyes for the week. Ava and Aaron were headed to France, though there were no buildings left, it was for the thrill and relaxation. Aine and Waya were on their way to Australia for the peaceful setting of Nature and scenery. Family and friends waved goodbye as the jets took off and disapeared into the horizon.

<hr>

Beyond the stars millions if lightyears away a small Earth-like planet rotates around a sun in its own quiet solar system. But the land below the atmosphere is far from quiet as its natives fight for their lives from the invaters that had landed just hours before. Large lizard-like creatures slaughter the planet's natives quickly as they slowly take over each ane every landmass. They communicate with one another in a thick German language simular to that of the threat that was sent to Earth. The Reptilian army quickly overwelled the natives and took the small planet a their own. Feeling victorious, the Reptilians sat in their ship and discussed future invations.

"I have a report from the planet Earth." One Reptilian said in a scratchy voice.

"Are the human in a panic still?" The General asked in a small laugh.

"Actually, they are trying to build ships that will save them. They plan on escaping."

"Don't you worry about that. Their progress will be far from done in the next two years. Their simple rocket science is nothing to fear. They are far behind where they could be."

"A...are you sure?" the ships on the scanner seem a bit more advanced than their normal."

"Never you worry. Just because they look like they would work, doesn't mean they will. They can't even comprehend how to create artificial gravity. On top of that, they would never have time to create hyperspace tech in such a short time. They are too simple minded for such things."

"You want me to call off the scout team?"

"For now yes. Wait until just before a month before our invation. Let them try their last attemp of survival. Let us focus on the invation we have next."

"As you wish sir. I shall send a message."

CHAPTER 11

It was New Years Eve of 2038 and a massive snowstorm has kept everyone locked safely in their warm tents for the past week. The Arc construction project has been put on hold for the season as of the first of december. Though has delayed progress, they were not put in a dangerous area of time due to them being ahead of schedual. The Arcs exteriors were complete and would begin the interiors come spring when trucks can get materials to their destinations. It has been almost a full nine months since the double wedding weekend and honeymoons.

Both Aine and Ava were nearing the end of their pregnancies, but the snowstorm has prevented much travel between their tents and the hospital tents. The wind blew hard outside as Aine and Waya sat at their table eating dinner that evening. Aine felt a pain and dropped her fork and held her stomach and caused Waya to look up at her in shock. He knew from the look on her face that something was wrong and that she was in pain. He got up from his seat and walked over to put his hands on her shoulders and kissed her head.

"Are you okay?" Waya asked concerned.

"I think my water just broke." Aine replied with a cringe.

"What? Already?" Waya paniced as he grabbed the phone.

"Yeah, it defenately broke." She replied as he dialed the hospital tent.

"ER, how may I help?" the front desk answered.

"It's Waya Aholoke. My wife just went into labor."

"I'll send an ambulance right away Mr. Aholoke."

"Thank you." Waya said and hung up. "An ambulance is on the way."

"Good to know." Aine replied. "Because I don't think I have very long."

"I hope you can last because of the storm outside delaying everything."
"If I can't, then you may have to deliver." Aine giggled.
"Don't say that! Don't even think it!" Waya joked nervously.

In the housing tent area, Ava and Aaron where in their tent number 63 having dinner when Ava began having small contractions as well. She was walking back to the table with her second helping of ribs, kraut, and potatos when the pain struck her. The pain caused her to drop her plate onto the tent floor as she grabbed her stomach and her water broke. When Aaron heared the crash, he rushed over and saw her squating over the puddle on the floor. He knew what this sight meant and he began to silently panic as he helped her to her feet.

"My water broke." Ava announced weakly.

"Okay, okay, I'll call for help. Hopfully they can get here through the storm."

"If not, then you will have to deliver our baby."

"Please don't say that. Im a tech not a doctor."

"You will be fine. Just relax and call for help." Ava giggled as Aaron dialed the number.

"Hello? Yeah hi um this is Aaron Bennet in tent 63, my wife, she um, her water broke."

"It's okay Mr. Bennet." Molly Price replied. "Help is on the way. Wow, this makes number two of the night."

"Help is on the way." Aaron said as he got off the phone. "Molly said you are number two of the night."

"I wonder if President Aholoke was the first." Ava replied. "She and I are at the same stage after all."

"That is a possibility. But lets just wonder and hope they make it in time."

"Why? So you won't have to deliver?" Ava giggled.

"Yes! Exactly!" Aaron freaked out a bit.

"Awe, my little nerd boy is scared and so fragile."

Anie and Waya were the first to arrive at the hospital tent that evening as it got darker and the storm became heavier. The storm blew out of control as the tent opened and and Aine entered on a hospital bed covered in many layers. As she sat up in the bed and it was wheeled into a room, Molly began preping her for delivery. Waya was siting in the waiting room while she was being preped as Ava arrived with Aaron. Once Aine was ready, Molly took Ava and began giving her the same treatment as Aaron sat beside Waya.

"You to huh?" Waya chuckled.

"Y-yeah." Was all Aaron could reply.

"Don't worry. Just because we are all living in tents at the moment, doesn't mean the tech is any less advanced than it was before. We have the best of the best here."

"I know. I just…. I'm not very good at this kind of thing." Aaron confessed.

"It sounds to me like Ava was your first everything." Waya joked and laughed, but Aaron stayed quiet. "Wait, are you serious?"

"I'm a programmer, not a socialist." Aaron blushed.

"It's all the same in the end. Esecially in this day in age. After all, it's people like you who are saving the world."

"Yeah, I've been working day and night on coding the database for each of the Arcs. I worry that I won't be around much for my kid due to my work. I feel as if I don't even give Ava enough attention." Aaron confessed in a concerned way.

"Now you sound like Aine." Waya chuckled. "The best we can do is just relax. After all, we are ahead of the Arc project."

"True, but the storm…"

"Is just a sidestep." Waya interrupted. "Trust me with the way everyone is working, we will be back on track in no time. The Arcs exteriors are complete and we will be starting on the interiors come spring. The goal was to be at 72% by this time and spend the winter with family. But we are way ahead of schedual. So relax a bit and spend time with your family."

"Okay, I'll try. What are you guys having anyway?"

"No try, do. And we want it to be a surprise."

"Wait, what?" Aaron raised an eyebrow, confused.

"You think you're the only nerd around here?" Waya joked.

"No, but Star Wars? Really?"

"It seems appropriate at this point. Doesn't it?" they both laughed.

"You two can go see your wives now." Molly announced as she walked into the room.

⸻

Aaron entered Ava's room cautiously while the doctor was doing his rounds of tests. There was a monitor beside the bed that read Ava and the baby's separate heartbeats. Her legs were proped up and spread while the doctor check how far down the baby had dropped. When Ava looked up and noticed Aaron walk in the room, she smiled and waved at him to be by her side. He sat down beside the bed and held her hand while the doctor finished his tests and changed gloves.

"You're not that far along." The doctor announced in a scratchy voice that matched his age. "When was your last contraction?"

"About twenty minutes ago when my water broke." Ava replied.

"Hmm, then you two are into a long night."

"How long of a night?" Aaron asked.

"Well, that is hard to say. But you two may have a New Years baby." Ava and Aaron looked at each other in silence. "I'll leave you to talk. I have to go check on Mrs. Aholoke." And with that, he left the room.

⸻

Aine's room was set up in a similar settint with a monitor connected to her and her legs hoisted up and spread. Waya was sitting beside the bed holding her hand when the doctor walked in and greeted them. He picked up the clipboard on her bed and reviewed her data on the sheet then sat down to her spread legs and administered his test. Once he was finished, he got up and stretched before changing his gloves for the next step.

"Well, just like Mrs. Bennet, you may also be in for a long night. When was your last contraction?"

"About a half hour ago." Aine replied.

"Well then, we will check on you and Ava every half hour until something changes. Watch some t.v. until then. You may even see the ball drop before the baby does." The doctor let out a hardy laugh at his own joke as he left the room.

Aine and Ava experienced contractions every half hour to forty-five minutes until eleven p.m. that night. Then they both started to have contractions every ten minutes as pain got more intense. Aine was the first to go into full labor as Dr. Ryan came in to do his rounds with the two. He had been delivering babies for the past twenty-five years and has had a perfect record with thouse who were in office. Aine and Ava would be another two knotches on his belt and he was happy to deliver the babies of the two women that had helped save the world.

"Seems as though you won't be seeing the ball drop." Dr. Ryan chuckled.

"Please just give me my shot." Was Aine's begging response.

"Very well, let's get you prepped. Molly will do the honors."

"There you are." Molly chirped as she poked Aine with the needle.

"OH GOD!" Ava shouted from the next room.

"Your shot is coming next hon." Molly replied as she changed the needle.

Ava was panting heavily as Molly entered the room with the syringe to give her the shot. Rolling her on her side, Molly administered the shot in her back to help her relax and a less painful delivery. Ava began to relax a bit once the shot kicked in but still felt the pressure as she took deep breaths. The snowstorm outside the hospital tent raged on as mindinight approched bringing the New Year and Two babies along with it.

* * *

"Push again." Dr. Ryan said calmly. "That's it, you're opening nicely." Aine screamed in pain as she pushed, what seemed like the hundreth time. "Okay good. Once more Aine, push. I see the head." She pushed once more and heard a cry as the baby slipped out. "Congratulations! It's a boy!"

"Hear that?" Waya asked. "We have a boy." He still held her hand and even with swollen fingers, he felt no pain.

"I'm tired Waya." Was Aine's only response as Dr. Ryan held the baby next to her for first contact.

"You get some sleep while the hospital patches you up and I take care of the rest." Aine nodded and dozed off.

"Twelve o'four." Dr. Ryan announced. "Happy New Year and Happy Birthday little man."

As Dr. Ryan walked out of the room with Waya and the new born boy, he heard Ava scream from the next room as Molly coached her. When he heared the struggle with no results, Dr. Ryan handed Waya his son and walked in to see Molly between Ava's legs and no sigh of the baby. She was panting and grunting with pain, but the baby wouldn't budge so he walked over to take a look. With a throbbing hand, Aaron held her hand and tried to stay calm with his wife's discomfort. At that moment, Dr. Ryan knew exactly what was wrong with the birthing prosses.

"Let me take a look please." Dr. Ryan said calmly. Molly let him take her place as she degloved. "I see, just as I thought. It's tangled."

"Tangled?" Aaron asked. "What do you mean tangled? Tangled on what?"

"The umbilical cord. Prep her for a c-section. The baby might be in danger."

"Danger?" Aaron freaked out.

"Calm down boy. I've done this a hundred time before without fail."

Two nurses rushed in with a divider sheet and helped Molly prep Ava for the c-section. Molly gave Ava one final shot as The two nurses finished prepping for Dr. Ryan to begin his job. He carefully, but quickly, used a scalpel to cut into Ava's belly and revealed the baby wrapped around its umbilical cord. He carefully unwrapped the baby and cut the cord from its body to set it free from its trap. Raising the infint up to the light, he smiled as it began to cry in his arms and he carried it to va's side for first contact.

"There we are little one." Dr. Ryan began. "No more wsorries. You are free and your mother is here with you. But she needs to rest."

"Is it safe now?" Aaron asked.

"Yes, and you have a healthy little girl."

"A girl? We have a girl? Ava, we have a girl!" Aaron sakd happily, but Ava was already asleep.

"let us clean the two infints and do our paperwork while the mothers' sleep. It has been a long night for everyone."

The two newborns were bathed, clothed, and tested while Aaron and Waya did the paperwork. Molly was in a room with Aaron as he filled out the paperwork for his and Ava's new daughter. She was asleep in the next room and he knew she would be out for the rest of the night. He didn't have to ask her about names because they had been dicussing possible names for a boy or a girl. The surprise was the best part of the wait and a baby girl was what they had received in return for their wait. A final name was decided for both a boy and a girl just hours before they entered the hospital during their dinner.

"And what will her name be?" Molly asked.

"Hope May Bennet." Aaron replied. "Our daughter's name is Hope, and hope is what she will breing."

"That's a lovely name for a new beginning."

"My wife and I discussed it for a long time and we know it will fit well."

"I'm sure it will. Now, since your baby girl was born on New Years Day, you will receive a care package with everything a baby needs for an entire year. This will apply with Waya and Aine's baby as well."

"Th-thank you. We gladly accept. I didn't know anyone did that."

While Aaron finished his paperwork, Molly entered the room that Waya was finishing his paperwork with a nurse fresh out of collage. Waya and Aine had a feeling that them may have a boy due to the symptoms and reactions. They knew from the start what they would name their boy when and if they had one, a name for a new beginning of humanity. It would be a name that would lead the Arc of humanity into the future that the people have always wanted but was out of reach until now.

"And what shall be his name Mr. Aholoke?" the nurse asked as Molly read through the paperwork.

"Noah Ray Aholoke." Waya replied happily.

"Oh, like Noah's Ark?"

"Exactly like Noah's Ark. Our people are at the point of going through a severe storm, not only the one outside, but the one coming in a little over a year from now. We have eighteen months before we have to finish our Arcs and my wife and I think it is appropriate for him to be named Noah."

"That is a lovely name Mr. Aholoke." Molly said, looking up. You know about the New Year's baby policy right?"

"Yes, of course, but you don't have to do that with us."

"It's the least we could do for all you have done for the world."

"Thank you very much Mrs. Price."

The blizzard outside raged on through the night while the New Year's Boy Noah and the Nea Year's Girl Hope were swaddled and laid into cribs beside their mothers'. Aine and Ava slept soundly in their beds with their husbands' beside them as full families. The winter was harsh and cold, but the love they had for ech other as a people now warmed the world more than ever before. Though the snow storm ragged on, they knew this was the calm before the true storm coming their way within the next eighteen months.

CHAPTER 12

Winter had come and gone as spring brought new life and eiger workers to continue construction on the Arc project. The multiple snowstorms had set them back, but not in a dangerous zone that could be fatal. Down south in the warm climates, people built interior parts of each Arc to get ready for transport. Being ahead of scedual before winter hit put them in a position where they could easily recover. Once the first warm day of spring came, the workers got back to work as the trucks began to arrive.

Sring also brung new life to the work that had to be done with everyone working harder than they ever had before. Layer after layer of the interior of each Arc was complete throughout the entire season. By the end of spring, the entire exterior was double layered for re-entry of their destination and the interior was ready for each floor to be built. Each floor would be used for different purposes from war to housing of the entire human race. Richard stood with his team of workers to give each group their jobs so that each floor could be built at the same time.

"Okay, first floor workers will be building the engine rooms for both blst off and travel." Richard began. "Second floor team will be working on the generators that will be used to send power throughout the Arc. The team that works on floors three through seven will build training and housing rooms for military use. This includes the docking stations for escape pods and space jets. The greenhouses will be on floors eight through twelve, which will be used for growing food for everyone on board throughout our journey. Next will be floors thirteen through eighteen, which will be used for markets, restaurants, and entertainment. There is no reason whe we shouldn't have to enjoy our travels. Floors nineteen through twenty-five will be built to house every citizen assigned to each Arc and will be the home to them throughout our journey. Last but not least will be floors twenty-six through thirty in wich will be our captian control bays. Each Arc will have its own captian and will be in charge of its occupupants. We have our orders, so lets get to work and put in some good time. We have fifteen months before we leave Earth behind. Lets make every monent count until then."

The workers made their way to their designated floors of each Arc to begin their most crucial job yet. Devided into several sections, elevators and platforms were set up to reach each area. On the first floor, or rather bottom of the Arc, Aaron helped set up the engins within the five sectional rooms. As each engine was placed into its place in each section, Aaron programed them with the codes he had created during the long winter. They were then connected to the exterior engins to be used for take-off, cruise control, and even hyper-drive.

The fifty engins for the Arcs were built during the down time in the winter by those who stayed in the south. Each one was the size of a small one story house and were bulted to the floor of the first floor in five different sections. They had been finished being built by the time spring came, but not programed by Aaron until they were placed into the Acrs. Heavy-duty cranes lifted each engin into the Arcs once they arrived in the semi trucks one at a time. Once each engin was connected to the exterior engins and Aaron hooked up his laptop to each ne to begin downloading the codes.

The second floor was divided into ten sections where massive generators, monitors, and basic utility access were to be placed. Each Arc was set up to have six generators to power their heat, AC, water, and electricity for everyone on board. The generators would also power the engins and monitors to make the Arcs eletric powered for more efficient travel and communication. Electricians and utility workers were among the main staff on this floor and would travel from their housing unites each day. As each generator was brought in, they were placed in their desiganted spot and connected to the monitors and intergrated into the walls to send electricity throughout the Arc. Once complete, Aaron would make his way to this floor to begin his coding into the generators and momitors.

Up on floors three through seven, construction workers began building training rooms and housing units for military personel and their families to live. Four of these five floors were divided into nine sections by rank for housing and training purposes. The seventh floor only had two sections for military machines and weapons while the other section was used for the bay to house the space jets to dock. Each floor had a docking station for escape pods that could hold up to three hundred people comfortably. Though the docking stations within these floors here ready to house their space fighter jets, they were still in development be Tristen and Vance were building.

The military training rooms were being built to withstand hardcore training for any upcoming battles. Armored walls and floors would make it easy to use explosives throughout their training. Right above them were the housing unites for the military families, this includes Naya and her children in their designated Arc. This floor was divided into two sections for housing and dinning rooms so that the residence wouldn't have to travel too far for what they need. As for the seventh floor of this section, it would be used for military intelligence and war planning.

On floors eight through twelve farmers, zookeepers, and landscapers began preparing these floors for Aaron's newly developed artifical atmosphere. Each floor would have its own environment to match the comfort for both plant and animal life that would live and grow there. Like the rest of the ship, the artifical gravity and atmosphere would be the crucial part of their journey through the great beyond. Once the landscaping is finished, all of Earth's seedlings would be transported to their designated floors to be stored for safe keeping. Along with Earth's plantlife, every animal species would also be transported to ensure their exsistance.

Moving up to floors thirteen through eighteen, we find the market area of the Arcs were stores, restaurants, and all types of entertainment possible. As the crops and farm animals are grown and raised below, they are brought here for everyone to dine on in the resaurants and gather in the markets built like super malls. All five floors are now being constructed with escalators and elevators for quick and easy access for the citizens. These six floors would soon be home to the freshed food, brand name supplies, and best entertainment that the world has to offer. Knowing that they could be living on the Arcs for quite awhile, they wanted to make the best of it.

Up above the market area, housing units for all citizens registered to each Arc start on floor nineteen and end on floor twenty-five. During the long winter, construction workers studied the blueprints that they were given of how many rooms each unit would have. Registration of every Arc was already complete and the units were planned out for each single or family of citizens. By this time, everyone knew what Arc number they were to be stationed and what housing unit number they would be in. each Arc had the same number as the one in the next, for example, Arc1: C-Unit12 or Arc2: C-Unit12 were their addresses. When it came to military units, the address would be different, such as Arc1: M-Unit12.

Last but not least, floors twenty-six through thirty were being built into three sections a piece. Floors twenty-six and twenty-seven were to be used for radar enviernment scanning for bio and electronical searches. Floors twenty-eight and twenty-nine consisted of communications between Arcs and broadcasting news reports. Finally, the thirtyith floor was the captain's bridge and control center for those who were registered to contol each Arc. This is where each captains, pilots, and main ship personnel would call home for the journey. This is also where the Arc's main computer and logbook were located for access.

<hr />

Mia and Tristen lay under the stars one warm summer day of the year 2039 as they finish off what was left of their two year anniversary day. They had exchanged gifts and spent the day relaxing and having fun without distractions from anyone. She had one more year of school left and would be free to choose her career as she pleased. They both knew what she wanted to do and had finally gotten up ythe nerve to tell her parents. To their surprise, they had already known what she wanted to do and accepted it with open arms.

"You knew that I race?" Mia asked, shocked.

"I treated your injuries." Her mother replied. "Of corse we knew. We just wanted you to tell us yourself."

"At first we didn't like it at all." He father joined in. "But we grew to trust Tristen and knew he was good for you. So, we let it go and let you be yourself instead of taking after one of us."

Mia was heartfelt for this information and she was glad that she was able to keep her dream out in the open. Her and Tristen had planned to find the first galatic racing competition once they arrive at their destination. Though it was excitiong, she knew they would need some other form of racing vehicle in order to enter a galatic race. She knew that their limited technology wouldn't do much for them against any other in the galaxy. They slepted away in each others arms as they dreamed of what the universe would be like once they did reach their destination.

It was now January of 2040 and all ten Arcs were nearly complete and ready for travel. Since it was the interior that the construction workers were building, nothing had stopped for the winter. Being ahead of schedual once again, all that remained was the transport of goods and ersonal belongings into the Arcs for their travels. Once thr crops were unloaded and the data was downloaded into the systems, a launch could be scedualed. Within the final stages of the Arcs developments, everyone was preparing for holidays, birthdays, and graduations befor the set summer travels. This would be the time for relaxation and celebration for all of humanity.

CHAPTER 13

The summer of 2040 had finally arrived and the ten Arcs were completely finished and ready for travel. Ava and Aaron Bennet prepare themselves for the next presidental announcement as crowds of people gather around. Behind Aine's podium was the site of Arc One in all its glory just waiting for its maiden voyage into the unknown. Pleased with their hard work and dedication, the crowd engaged in conversation with one another as they awaited the next phase in the plan from President Aine O'Conner Aholoke. Excitement with a tinge of fear had filled the air of the upcoming travels through the great beyond.

"In three, two, one..." Aaron counted down as Ava stepped in front of the camera.

"Greetings to all on this wounderful summer day." Ava began. "As you all know, all ten Arcs have recently been completed and are ready for lift off. Behind me is the site of Arc One, future home to Presidental couple Aine and Waya Aholoke and several of you as well. Today, Aine Aholoke will announce the next phase in the relocation plan, along with what we had discovered recently beyond the stars. I will transfer you over now."

As the report was being transferred to the next camera, Aine entered the scene with a pleased look on her face while smiling and waving to the crowd. When the crowd saw her walk to the podium, they erupted with cheer and excitement. They knew this speech would be history in the making and that soon the human race will go farther than they had ever gone before. Aine stood at the podium and stared into the crowd with goosebumps covering every inch of her body. She was about to give the greatest speech in human history and help lead them into a grand future.

"Good morning Earth!" Aine shouted with glee and the crowd erupted with cheer once again. "Today is a grand day for the human race. This is the day that all ten Arcs are fully complete and ready for their maiden voyage. Today also marks a day in our history and future of how well we all put our differences aside and worked together to create peace and freedom for all. For decades humanity has faught to reach the stars devided. Though we did accomplish much individually, nothing compares to what we have just accomplished now.we have accomplished more as one people in the last three years than we have as separate nations in the last eighty years. Behind me not only sits the future of our existence, but also the future of many more accomplishments. This is only the first step in many things we can do as one. We have proven that we can overcome our greatest weaknesses and do anything. In three weeks time marks the day three years ago that we recived the horrifying message that threatened our very exsistence. Now we not only have a way to escape, but to also fight back. Though our technology is still behind, our world military is much stronger now. We will live one, for in one week we will be celebrating the final graduation on Earth. Following that day, we will set a course into the great beyond and a new horizon. We shall be long gone before our enemy has a chance to reach our planet and gain allies within the galaxy to fight them if we ever need to."

Once again, the crowd roard cheerfully when Aine finished her speech for everything that her and Waya had done for them. In one week's time they would be resting in their housing units as they journey safely through the stars. As the crowd calmed down and disperse, they stopped in their tracks as Mia unexpectedly made her way to the podium. Aine was just as surprised to see her approch without any warning and take the mike in her hand. Silence filled the air as she stood in front of the crowd with her eyes closed and her head down.

Suddenly without any warning, Mia began to sing into the mike and the crowed watched in shock. Her voice filled the air with the sound of love and truth as everyone closed their eyes and opened their hearts to the words. Nobody had expected her to be able to sing in such a way, nor did they expect her to be breave enough to sing in front of a camera. Once she was finished, the crowd roared for her and knew the reason why she chose such a song for the world to hear. She smiled and ran into Tristen's arms and made her way through the crowd as they all contenued to cheer for her.

With cheerful smiles and hearts, everyone began to set up rides and concession stands to celebrate with a festival. Music played over the loud speakers that were attached the the Arcs and game stands were set up with several prizes to win. No money was used for the festival for this wasn't for a profit, instead it was for the the celebration of life and the second chance they were all given. A city-wide stretch of land the size of Los Angeles was made into the largest fairground location with millions of eople coming and going throughout the festival. The entire human race had finally arrived at the Arc site within the first day of the celebration and began entering their scedualed Arcs.

Three days into the the festival and it was still going strong with food, games, and rides. Music played constently and when each day was done, everyone made their way to their housing units aboard the Arcs. Mia and Tristen entered the fairgrounds each day holding hands for this was the longest time they got to spend together throughout the last three years. They had spent every availible moment together since the racing accident and had became a very close couple dispite the construction project. Now that Mia was eighteen and about to graduate within the week, she had been thinking of the career she would choose.

Tristen had convince her to come to the festival in order to clear her head knowing she was stressed about the choice. Her family had known about her racing and had let her make her choice, but she knew they wanted her to choose a better life career to fall back on. Both Tristen and Mia's dream was to enter the greatest race in the galaxy, but he had a military career and she had no other ideas for life. Though she could sing and everyone praised her for it, she douted that it would be the type of career she could fall back on.

"See, I told you this was relaxing." Tristen announced as he handed her a funnel cake.

"Yeah, I guess." Mia replied. "I just don't know what I want to do. I just know that I DON'T want to be a nurse or build rockets for a living."

"I know you love to race. I love it to and the money was good before the message, but we don't know how that money will turn out elsewhere in the galaxy."

"Is that why you went into the military and became a pilot?"

"I chose this career when I was younger knowing I couldn't always live off of racing money because times were changing. Plus I got to put my skills to the test this way."

"What skills are those?" Mia joked.

"Funny." Tristen rolled his eyes. "I could beat you any day of the week."

"Put your money where your mouth is bud."

"I'll make you a deal. Relax today at the festival and stop thinking of your future and I'll race you tonight."

"Y-you promise?"

"Yes, I promise. Besides, I have a surprise for you anyway."

"Woo hoo! You're on."

Mia grabbed his hand and rushed him towards the rides and he couldn't help but laugh. The day faded into night while everyone enjoyed themselves and cleared their minds of what the future held for them. Mia and Tristen made their way from the fairgrounds and towards the Arc bay garages. Quietly, they opened the door and snuck inside as Tristen hit the lights and lit up the room to a surprise. Mia's eyes lit up when she saw two newly built chargers sitting side by side and squeeled. She noticed that they were much different than the normal design and didn't seem to show the wheels. Two rocket engines were in the back where the mufflers would normally go and a fully flat bottom.

"What.... What is this?" Mia asked, shocked.

"These are newly developed star racers." Tristen replied. "You see, the crew that I lead during the construction project helped me built them. They were built from scratch using the escape pod blueprints along with the charger design. Since I was in charge of building the escape pods, I had access to all of the equioment required to build them."

"That's amazing! When did you finish them?"

"Last week we put the final touches on them. But I waited until now for two reasons. One, because of the Arcs and two because today markes our three year anniversary."

"You built me a star racer for our anniversary gift? So this is what you were doing when you told me you wanted to race among the stars."

"It has always been a dream of mine. Now, I will teach you how to fly as a racer and a pilot."

Getting into the driver's seat, Mia noticed that the wheel was that of a jet for steering. Since the racer was designed to hover and fly, she knew it made sense to build this kind of feature. Most of the interior of the racer was basic and designed as if it was a nomal vehicle for tavel but with jet fighter controles and flight technology. She laied her head back in the seat and thought about the kind of races she would be joining in this racer. She knew there was no way she could race him tonight because she didn't know how to fly. He would have to teach her how to control the racer and she knew it would take the entire time they had left in order to learn the basics.

Deep in space millions of lightyears away, a reptilian army ripped through a less advanced race and dominated them. The message came through just as the general that lead this fleet made his way to the leader's building. Anger filled him as her listened to the report of the human Arcs and the scedualed liftoff. This was his mission and the fact that they had worked together so suddenly and accomplished what he told his leaders not to worry about, burned him. He dropped what he was doing and left his most trusted soldier in charge of the takeover.

As he got aboard his ship, he lead a small fleet away from the battle on the planet below. This small fleet of five battleships followed the General as he traveled a safe distance from the planet below. Once the five ships were a safe distance away from the full invastion fleet, the general and his five ships entered hyperspace to travel to Earth in order to stop the retreat. He knew they all must die or it would be his head for failing such an important mission. Anger and rage filled him as they traveled knowing it would take a few days to reach Earth even through hyperspace. The human race had no idea what dangers made their way to them as they partied on in a grand celebration.

CHAPTER 14

The sun began to rise high in the sky the day of the final graduation ceremonies one week from the day the festival started. High school and collage graduations were happening in several locations outside the Arc sites. High school seniors were getting their deplomas while many collage students were getting their degrees. Among these groups was Mia Price, an eighteen year old high school senior who has yet to find her true path. Her parents knew she was a racer and could sing, but didn't want this to be her only path in life. They wanted her to choose a path in a collage or tech school even if it wasn't in the same field as they were.

Mia lined up with the other students as the crowd gathered around and the teachers sat behind the podium. Each student sat in a line side by side on the stage looking down at their families below. They all sat in alphabetical order by last name so that each one could stand and receive their deploma as their names were called. Mia's family sat in the crowd watching along with Tristen, who was holding a camcorder, as the principal called out each name. the principal read off each name until he got to the P section on the name list and Mia knew she was soon to be next.

"Price, Mia Price." The principal called out as her family cheered.

"Speech, speech, speech." Ritchard called out as Mia took her diploma.

"Oh god…. Um…" Mia replied as she took her diploma. "Well um…. I guess to tell you the truth, I'm surprised that I made it this far. I know that I'm no rocket scientist like my dad." The crowd laughed at her somewhat serious joke. "But to be honest, I still don't know what I want to do now that I graduated. All I know is that I don't want to be the typical career like a doctor or build rockets or even military vehicles." Her family looked at each other confused with her statement. "Maybe I'll be a perfessional race car driver or singer. With everything that has been going on the past three years, I just don't know until we get settled in a new place. I just want to focus on the now. That's the bast I can do. Who knows what new opportunities we will have later. So I just want to wait and see what life brings."

The crowd went silent and her family sank into their seats knowing she was right to see what the future brings. New technology from new worlds will upgrade many opportunities for everyone weather its for medical or computers. Mia knew she may get a three on one lecture later if she kept her speech going so she ended it there. Racing was all she knew and everyone knew that it was what she loved to do most so it made sense to them that she would say so now. She loved the feeling of the vibration as the motor revved up along with the thrill of the seed and danger with every race.

Being behind the wheel and feeling free was her favorate part of the experience and she wouldn't give it up for anything in the world. These things among much, much more is what Mia needed, wanted, and craved in her young life. But she only found these things while being beside Tristen and being behind the wheel of a racer. Her family knew this of her and knew she ment what she said about being a racer even though it came out as a joke. They accepted her choice and just wanted her to be happy with whatever life she chose to have.

As Mia walked off the stage, the principal called out the next name on the list after a moment of hesitation. Tristen knew what she had ment by what she said with life and confusing choices for any life-long decision was difficult to make not knowing if the choice you make would be worth it in the end even if it made you happy. He knew she was a racer at heart from the first time he watched her and knew it would always be the path she would turn to reguardless of what other people thought. Though he hated to admit it, he knew she was better than him in every way from respecting her family's dicisions and admitting the faults in her own dicisions. She was even a better racer because the thought back to the crashe that he caused and avoided racing her every chance he got not only from the guilt but because he knew she would beat him easily.

Mia sat down next to Tristen and watched the rest of the graduation ceremony with him and her family. The sun was high and it was just about lunch time when it was all over and everyone began to disperse from the area. Food stand from the festival were the only things still up and running for those who were organizing their housing units in the Arcs. The rides and game stands were dismantaled and transported into the Arcs the day before when the festival ended. One by one, each graduation ceremony ended and everyone grabbed lunch before dismantaling the stands and moving them to the Arcs.

Mia, her family, and Tristen made their way to Arc One where they were registered to stay. This was also the home to Aine, Waya, and Noah Aholoke for the duration of their trip. Each Arc had its own Captain and Aine was the Captain of Arc One where Ronny Davis was named the Captain on Arc Two. Along with him, Naya, Jason, and Arial were registered to this Arc during the journey through the stars. Each resident of each Arc had an housing unit with their own address they were registered to.

Each group entered the Arcs in elevators that took them to the housing floors of nineteen through twenty-five. In Arc One, Mia and her family were ragistered to Arc1: C-Unit 584 other than Vance who was registered to Arc:1 M-Unit 72. Tristen was also registered to the military units of Arc1: M-Unit 76 due to their military status'. Naya and her children were registered in the address of Arc2: C-Unit 416 since they were citizens and no longer under the military base registration. This did not bother them or Ronny knowing they would be safe reguardless of the situation.

The Arcs were set up like cities in order to make it easy for everyone to find their way around weather it was in the market areas or housing units. Every housing unit had a card key to enter with like a hotel key for sucerity perpouses. Ritchard Price swipped his unit card and entered the unit along with his family after a long day. The interior of the unit was built and looked simular to their San Francisco home design with a second floor attached. With all of their belonging already inside, they were ready to unpack and organize their new home before the launch time arrived.

"Before we unpack and organize our unit," Ritchard began. "Let's talk about your speech today Mia."

'And here we go.' Mia thought to herself. "Look dad, I don't know what I want to do. I just know that I don't want to be like any of you."

"What's wrong with us?" Molly asked.

"Nothing. I just don't want to cut people open or give them shots. And I don't like rocket science and I don't want to build or fix anything unless it is my own car."

"Become a mechanic." Vance chimed in.

"I said my own car." Mia grumbbled. "I'm not going through school just to spend all day changing oil and fixing bumpers for chump change."

"Mia!" Molly replied, shocked.

"Well it's true. I just don't know what I want to do right now. Can't we just leave it at that for now?"

"We can." Ritchard replied. "But all we wanted to talk about was that we accept your decision because we wouldn't want you to be overwhelmed during the travel. we know that things will be different and that there will be more opportunities later on."

"Plus we don't mind if you race." Vance added. "As long as it is in a legal way."

"Thank you." Mia replied. "That's all I wanted. I'm tired so I'm going to take a nap until we launch."

That was all that could be said before Mia ran upstairs to her room to escape any more of the conversation with her family. Inside the room, the walls and bed were barewith new sheets and blankets folded neatly on the chest at the foot of the bed. The room was about the same size as the one from her family home back in California. In the corner of the room was a stack of boxes with all of her belongings incuding posters, clothes, and collectables. It had been a long day for her as she sat down on the bed not feeling like unpacking or organizing anything.

But what she did feel like doing was going on a long drive or having a competitive race with someone. That was something that she couldn't do until they had arrived wherever they were headed due to the size of the walkways of the ship. Though it was a large city-sized ship with plenty of room to travel, they did not build roads for anyone to use because all vehicles were taken apart to build escape pods and other parts of the ships. The only two citizen type vehicles left were the star racers that Tristen and his team secretly built. So, she reached out and grabbed her blanket and held it close to herself thinking that if she couldet drive or at least see Tristen until after the launch, she would just sleep.

Outside the Arc sites, billions of people gathered around their designated Arc as they boarded the massive ships. From sea to sea, country to country the land looked bare and uninhabited by both humans and animals. Though there were a few groups of wild animals around, they seemed to be endangered due to the amout of them. Everyone knew they would survive and breed safely as the Earth began to heal from the lack of human inhabbitince. The Earth hadn't looked as bare as it did now since prehistoric times when mamles first began to emerge and take over.

These were the deep thoughts of Aine Aholoke as she watched everyone board the Arcs through the window of the Captain's Bridge. Both her and Waya had two back-up plans in place just in case things went sour upon leaving Earth behind. Knowing that they were leaving two weeks ahead of schedual, the felt safe from the harm that their enemy could inflict upon them. Both plans stayed in place for the future to insure their safe tavels to a new world and a better hope for all of humanity. Aine closed her eyes and sighed deeply with both concern and relief as she watched the last of the citizens boarded the ships below.

By the time the sunset began, the last of the boarders made their way to their units to await the launch of the ten Arcs. Ava and Aaron entered their unit of Arc2: C-Unit 317 with their daughter Hope and instently laid her down for the night. Once they had gotten her to sleep, they began to unpack and organize their belongings throughout the unit. Aaron put his camera next to the laptop to do editing later of everything they had recorded of the day. They had videoed the final moments they would spend on Earth and the boarding event for future generations to watch. Their main goal was to record their entire journey so that the historical events could be viewed by the future generations of humanity in schools.

Naya, Jason, and Arial boarded Arc Two with Ronny and made their way to unit Arc2: C-Unit 142 to prepare themselves for the launch. They had left Ronny on the elevator as he made his way to the Captian's bridge in order to make contatct with the other Arcs. Arc Two was his reponsibility given to him by Aine and Waya to take care of during the long journey. This would be his greatest mission and achievment yet he thought to himself as he entered the bridge. But the last thought that had entered his mind as he contacted the other Arcs was that this would be the last day humanity would inhabbit Earth.

All ten Arcs began to be switched on in order to warm up the engines for their maiden voyage. Everyone of Earth's inhabbitence were safely in their units with their families awaiting the announcement of their leader Aine Aholoke. As the engines revved up, the children watched the sunset out their windows while each Arc captian prepared their communications. Every system was on including the newly developed artificial atmosphere of the ship to insure that each passenger would be comfortable duing the move. By this time, everyone was thinking the same thing that this was Earth's farewell to its native species and a new horizon would be seen in the near future.

CHAPTER 15

It was 8 p.m. when Aine Aholoke's voice sounded over the intercom systems within each housing unit for both citizens and military staff. Those whe were taking a nap and awaiting the message, woke up in excitement from the president's call. Those whe were unpacking and organizing their belongings, dropped what they were doing and made their ways to the living room. Each family grouped together in anticipation to listen to Aine's announcement. The time had finally come for the ten Arcs to launch into space and journey into the stars.

"Good evening to you all." Aine's voice rang out. "We will be launching in key minus twenty minutes. The liftoff may get a little bumpy so please stick together and prepare yourselves for the ride. Once we are safely in Earth's orbit, you will be free to move around the ship and do as you please while the ship gets prepared for hyperspace. The journey will take a few days but at least we will be safely out of harms way. There has been no word from our enemy as of yet and we are two weeks ahead of launching schedual so it seems that we are in the clear. I will make another anoucement when we reach Earth's orbit and let you know that it is safe."

Once the announcement had ended, everyone began to prepare for a bumpy launch out of the atmosphere. The sofas inside each unit had built-in seatbelts so that the citizens could be safe during the launch and hyperdrive activation. Aine made her way to the control center of the captian's bridge to check on the launce status. All computers were lit up with numbers and codes along with blinking lights of every color. Each computer station had its own person monitoring the screens and control pannels.

"Is everything ready?" Aine asked.

"Yes ma'am." The two pilots answered in sink.

"Engines are fully charged and ready to go." A young woman behind a control pannel announced.

The room was similar to a NASA control room with long desks with computers and control pannels lined up in rows. Each Arc had two pilots that steered the ships and used two separate levers to begin moving along thr road. The Arcs were automaticlly detached from the towers as it made their way down the ten long roads and picking up speed. One by one, switches were turned and buttons pressed as the ten Arcs bolted down the roads like bullet trains. Everyone began to buckle themselves in as they prepared for their ascent out of the atmosphere.

"Eighty knots, one hundred knots, one hundred and twenty knots." The pilots shouted as the engines roared loudly.

"Good." Aine replied. "Keep it up team, we are almost there."

Down below each Arc, several workers on the first floor monitored the engines and ware earplugs as they roared loudly. They made sure that each one stayed in sink with one another and that the back-ups were fully charged and functional. The engine rooms began to heat up from the startup and air conditioners kicked on to cool down both the workers and engines to insure that the personel and ships were safe during liftoff. By the readings on the monitors, everything was going smoothly, but they knew that this was only the beginning of a very long launch and journey. Everything had to be in perfect sink because this wasn't just the maiden voyage of the Arcs, but also of the human race for their tavel outsid their own solar system.

Up on the second floor, the power generators were running at full capasity with multiple werkers manitoring every inch of the gigantic machines to make sure they were working properly. Power gages were raised and lowered in sequince during the time the Arcs were picking up speed. Lights dimmed throughout the Arcs as they gave energy to the machines while they prepared for the first launch. Strapped into chairs that were bolted to the ground, the workers tierlessly keeped the generatorsat full capasity. They last thing they needed was apower outage during or after launch into space.

"Arc One is at full speed and capasity Madam President." Pilot one announced.

"Excellent." Aine replied. "Begin liftoff."

"Beginning liftoff.: Pilot two replied.

The back engines began to charge like those of a fighter jet as each Arc began to lift themselves off the ground like massive city-sized blimps. As the Arcs gained altitude, turbulence began to take effect like that of a normal flight on an airlinner. Families stayed huddled together on their seatbelted sofas in their units as the liftoff proceeded. On floor eight through twelve, trees shook from the turbulence and the animals began to freak out from the sudden quaking. Farmers, ranchers, and zookeepers did everything could to keep the animals calm during the quaking liftoff. Citizens were holding onto each other as the Arcs quaked, rumbled, and bounced.

"We are now three miles above the launch site Madam President." Pilot one announced.

"We are now entering atmospheric pressure." Pilot two added.

"How long until we reach orbit hight?" Aine asked.

"At this rate, about fifteen minutes max." Pilot two replied.

"Once we do enter the orbit hight, we will have to let the hyperdrive engines charge for fourty-five minutes before it can be used." Pilot one said.

"Very well." Aine said, pleased. "Once we reach orbit hight, activate the speekers for my announcement."

Both pilots activated the atmospheric presure shields as the Arcs pushed through each layer. The surroundings outside the Arcs began to get darker as they neared their orbit destination. The Arcs pushed harder and harder through the troposphere, stratosphere, mesosphere, thermosphere and finally the exosphere. Soon the only light was from the Arcs as they reached orbit and the main engines began to cut off. Once the engines were fully off and the rumbling ships stopped in the black of space, the captain's bridge techs activated the artificial gravity so that the citizens and animals could safely walk on the ground.

This was recent technology to humanity but with the greatest minds working together, it was a success, and it was like walking on the surface of Earth. It was the first time for anyone on the ten Arcs to see space in this way and it was hard for anyone to look away. Even those who were the control rooms couldn't help but stare deep into the vastness of space. On the first floor of each Arc the workers began to refuel the massive tanks so that the ships could recharge and get ready for the first hyperspace trip.

Everyone only stopped what they were doing when Aine came over the intercom with her next announcement.

"All systems are steady and normal." Pilot one exclaimed. "The launch was a complete success."

"Great job everyone." Aine replied and everyone began to cheer.

"Shutting down and recharging now." Pilot two chimed in. "In about five minutes, we can begin charging the hyperdrive."

"Good to hear." Aine said. "Are we still able to communicate with the other Arcs?"

"Yes ma'am." A woman from communications replied. "I'll patch you through now."

"Before you do, I want to make an announcement to our Arc citizens first." Communications complied and turned on the intercom.

"I am proud to announce that we have successfully made our way to orbit." Aine announced over the intercom. "We are now charging the Arcs for hyperdrive and will be leaving Earth behind in a little less than an hour. If you would like, you are free to roam around outside your units until my announcement when this happens. Thank you all for your arduous work and cooperation."

Once Aine's announcement was over, communications began connecting Arc One with the other Arcs for a full meeting with the other captains. A large screen lowered in front of her as a video message began and one by one each captain from the other Arcs began to appear on screen including Ronny Davis from Arc Two. Though the ride had been rough on the way to orbit, the captains of each Arc stood steady and strong as they awaited the start of the meeting.

"How did your Arcs manage through liftoff?" Aine asked.

"We are good on this end." Ronny replied from Arc Two and the rest followed suit.

"Good to hear. Let us start charging the engines and hyperdrive because we will be engaging them within the hour.

While the hyperdrive and engines charged, everyone began to relax and plan out their next step through the voyage. Ronny excused himself from the bridge in order to check on Naya and the kids to make sure they had a safe launch. After losing their father and husband, Ronny felt a need to protect them any way he could. Though he loves Naya, he thinks of her as a little sister and that alone makes him feel responsible for her, Jason, and Arial. He made his way down the hallway to their unit in the family section of Arc to and knocked on the door.

"I knew you couldn't resist checking up on us." Naya giggled as she opened the door.

"Can you blame me?" Ronny teased. "You're so fragile."

"I'm tougher than you give me credit for you know." This made them both laugh out loud.

"Come on." Ronny said. "We launch the hyperdrive in less than an hour and I want to show you the bridge."

"Isn't that against the rules?"

"I'm the captain of this ship and I make the rules." Naya grinned wildly and called for the kids to follow.

On Arc One, Mia lays in her bed as the announcement from President Aine Aholoke ends. She lays in silence for a moment as she thinks of everything that has happened the last three years and where her life is now headed. Though the voyage gives her a break from talking to her parents about her future, the thoughts of what she truly wants to do with her life nips at her brain. Her family knows that she races and accepts this part of her life, but she knows that they want her to do more. She also knows that Tristen has chose a secondary career in the military along side his racing and now she wonders about what she could do as well.

Her thoughts lead her back to the day she had sang in front of hundreds of thousands of people before she even graduated. Tristen was the only one who had knew she could sing and had promised to keep it a secret until she was ready to tell others herself. Though after he had witnessed her sing and spied until she was finished before making himself known to her, he respected her wishes and kept it to himself. She often wondered if singing was an optional career for her, but would her parents accept that, or would they see it like the saw her racing? The thoughts made her angry and she shooed them away as she lifted herself out of bed and down the stairs.

"Since we have time," Mia announced as she entered the living room. "I'm going to visit with Tristen until we launch the hyperdrive."

"Okay." Molly replied. "Just don't be gone to long." Mia knotted as she closed the door.

Mia made her way to the elevator and to the military housing floors where Tristen's unit was. The though of entering the military to be closer to him crossed her mind as she walked down the long hallway. The training would be worth it, and it way even make her parents settle down on her making a decision. The only flaw to this would be that she would have no choice but to be sent into battle and wouldn't have a true life of her own. The though clouded her but the cloud faded as she reached Tristen's door and knocked.

"Aren't you supposed to be huddling with your family right now?" Tristen teased as he opened the door with a raised eyebrow.

"I'd rather be huddling with you instead." Mia replied with a wicked smile.

"What kind of books have you been reading in order to come up with that freaky comment?"

"Wouldn't you like to know." Mia giggled. "Now are you going to invite me in or not?" He moved and let her pass through the doorway as the door closed and locked behind them.

On Arc two, Ava and Aaron were already on the bridge when Ronny arrived with Naya, Jason, and Arial. They were recording the unlimited view of space and documenting their surroundings for their documentary reports. As they were filming shooting stars, floating debris, and old satellites, something caught Aaron's eye and he zoomed in to get a better look. Once Ronny, Naya, and the kids reached them, Aaron's eyes were wide with shock, interest, and fear. He hadn't even noticed when Ronny and Ava began to speak with one another as he stared into the mysterious object in space.

"Get any good shots?" Ronny asked.

"Yeah." Ava cheered. "Great stuff for our documents. Thanks for letting us come up here Uncle Ronny."

"No problem. You're welcome. You are always welcome here. How is hope doing? Did the launch go well for her?"

"Yeah, she slept right through it and is still sleeping."

"Um…. Guys." Aaron said with a shaky voice. "I don't know what kind it is, but it looks as though a hole is opening up in front of us."

"That's no ordinary hole sir." One of the surrounding scanner personal announced. "According to the readings, something is about to exit hyperspace."

With those few simple words, fear began to emerge from everyone in the room as they watched the hundreds of colors form in front of their eyes in the dead of space. They knew in their hearts what this meant and there was no way they could escape when the hyperdrive was just starting to charge. They were also stuck in place because the regular engines were beginning to recharge and being refilled for travel. The only thing that went through their minds weas that they were trapped for the next hour with nowhere to run or hide.

CHAPTER 16

Aine was frozen with fear as she witnessed the hole in hyperspace begin to open and shift. Her whole body ached and shivered as goosebumps began to form on every inch of her now pale skin. The blood had completely drained from her as she watched in horror of the events that she knew they could not escape from or stand a chance to fight against at this time. Then, all her fears came to light as five large ships began to emerge from the massive hole in space in front of their eyes. Four of them were the size of one Arc and the fifth was the size of three of them combined.

The ships had an eerie look to them with a light green shade and spiked back end as if it was a lizard's tale. The front ends looked like the head of a Komodo Dragon with red tinted widows that looked like eyes. The five ships came to a dead stop in front of their ten Arcs, with the largest of them in the front and two smaller ships on each side making them look like an arrowhead. Its was so silent with no movement that it was as if there was a stalemate between the two with each side waiting for the other to make the first move. After several moments had past and nobody dared to move a single muscle, a red light began to bleep on the video monitor with a soft alarm indicating that there was an exterior call coming in.

"Incoming transmission from the new arrivals Mrs. President." A woman in communications announced.

"Go ahead and put them through." Aine replied. "I want to hear what they have say and maybe talk our way through a safe passage out of here."

"Yes ma'am. Putting them through now."

As communications patched the enemy ship through, the other Arcs called in and the nine screens appeared on the screen. Then a tenth screen appeared to where every Arc was capable of seeing and hearing what was about to unfold. Everyone braced themselves for the alien that they would see for the first time since the horrific message from three years back. When the creature appeared in front of the screen, Ronny and Naya, along with all the others that could see the monitor, were horrified by the site that their eyes had witnessed. Aaron had been right when his research led him and others to believe that the aliens that had sent the message was in the reptilian category of creatures.

On the screen appeared a lizard-like creature with dark green skin that stood upright on its long muscular hind legs. Its head was round on top with a long snout along with the back of its head with horn-like pikes in the back, much like the ship it had arrived in. the creature's eyes were a dark shade of yellow that showed hatred with no hint of forgiveness or mercy. Its mouth held what looked like hundreds of razer-sharp teeth and a split tongue, much like and reptilian. It had a bulk, muscular body that was covered in armor that was gold in color with spiked shoulders. Its long tail was free armor and swayed from side to side as it raised its head with a smile as it began to speak.

"Greeting's humans." The reptile spoke in a raspy voice. Aine and Ronny shivered when they recognized the voice of the one that had sent the threatening message three years prior. "I see you are taking your leave from this little rock of yours."

"We don't want any trouble." Aine said as calmly as she could while trembling. "You may have Earth if that is what you want. All we ask is that you let us pass safely."

"I must confess, I hadn't expected your species to get so far in such a short amount of time."

"Desperate times call for desperate measures."

"I suppose so. I have been watching you for quite some time and we couldn't resist seeing you off."

"So, you're going to let us pass then?"

"That is not what I meant." The alien hissed angerly as he squinted his eyes.

"We wish to avoid a fight." Aine pressed a little more sternly. "All we wish to do is leave Earth behind. Is there any way we can resolve this situation peacefully?"

"You just don't get it do you?" The reptile laughed gruffly. "I meant what I said about your pitiful race being worthless to the universe. We

was the third-floor docking bays where the space fighter jets were docked and ready for battle. Tristen and Mia held each other's hands tightly as the elevator made its way down to the third floor. When the elevator came to a stop and the door opened, they ran through the docking bay passing hundreds of jets lined up, side by side. Tristen's commanding officer was talking to a group of pilots and giving them orders when they reached him.

"Aaron," Aine called out. "What percentage do we need for a safe jump into hyperspace?"

"At least 85% Mrs. President." Aaron replied from behind Ronny on Arc two. "That is the minimum we can do with a first attempt."

"How long will it take to get to that point? We are about to engage in battle."

"About thirty-five minutes. We are at 10% now and raising. But I can see what I can do to speed up the prosses."

"I'm counting on you Aaron. Ronny, get your best forces out there and give them hell. We must protect the Arcs as much as we can for the next thirty-five minutes. That goes for the rest of you on every Arc. Let's give them hell."

"Aye Captain." Ronny replied with a salute and a smirk.

"Let's show them our bluff. No matter the outcome of this battle, it will look as if Earth can't be used anymore."

Aaron logged onto the 'bluff plan' on his computer screen and sent a signal from Arc Two towards Earth that connected to each and every satellite that orbited the planet. The system activated and Earth looked as if it began to rumble as dark grey smoke consumed the atmosphere. Though humanity knew that this was only a hologram, but the reptilians would see this as if every nuke had been released on the surface of Earth and now killing everything that could be of use. The great blue planet now looked like nothing more than a grey and green ball floating in space. Aine knew that the bluff had worked when the first attack came instantaneously from the largest of the five enemy ships.

She knew that the war had started three years back before their enemy had revealed themselves and that there was no talking themselves out of the inevitable. At this point, it was all or nothing until the hyper-drive was charged enough for a jump that could save the existence of humanity. If they could not hold their own for just thirty-five minutes, then may not be able to survive what was waiting for them on the other side of the jump. But nothing could have prepared her or anyone for the attack that was about to be unleashed onto them from the savage cold-blooded beasts before them. Fear consumed her as she witnessed the horror of ship in front of her as it opened its mouth-shaped front to reveal what could be the end of them all.

The jaw lowered to reveal a large cylinder tube that was engulfed by and electrical current as it began to charge for an ultimate attack. Aine fell to her knees trembling, as the Mothership aimed its primary weapon at Arc Five and a massive light lit up the blackness of space like a nova and fired point blank. Before the laser even hit the Arc, the pure force of the attack sent a massive shockwave through the surrounding areas that made the other Arcs rumble like an Earthquake. The electrical laser hit Arc Five with so much force that it cut through the dead center of its captain's bridge and began to immediately begun to explode on contact from the inside out. Aine watched in horror as 7.5 million people were instantly wiped out and she knew that thirty-five minutes was too long of a wait for their entire species could be completely incinerated with only nine more of these lasers.

CHAPTER 17

Mia and Tristen fell to the floor with the rest of the pilots in docking bay five as the massive shockwave shook Arc One. None of the jets were damaged during the first attack, but Mia was frozen with terror as she watched Arc Five get obliterated outside the Bay window. Hoping that the Mothership would have to charge a great deal of time to send out another attack like that again, they lifted to their feet and tried to calm themselves down. The commander then noticed Mia standing beside Tristen and did not seem to be in a good mood to see her in the bay. He was a beast of a man who looked like he hasn't seen a good day since he was a very young child.

"Who is this?" The commander growled bluntly without hesitation.

"This is Mia sir." Tristen replied calmly. She is my girlfriend and…"

"She doesn't belong here." The brute interrupted.

"No offense sir, but this is no time to argue of stay within rank. I have been training her to fly myself."

The commander looked Mia up and down to study her and then back at the bay window to look at the floating remains of Arc Five. "Fine, but don't do anything stupid. I won't babysit you."

"Come on." Tristen smiled. "It's me you're talking about."

"That's what I mean. Now take eagles seven and eight."

"Yes sir, thank you sir."

Tristen sprinted down the bay hangers with Mia close and neither of them spoke until they were out of ear shot of the commander. "You used my line." Mia grinned.

"Sometimes you actually make a good point." Tristen replied sarcastically.

"Hey! More than you most of the time."

"This is Eagle Eight." Tristen Stopped and gave a large red jet a pat. "The one next to it is Eagle Seven, that one is yours so hop in and let's go."

"This is really happening, isn't it?" Mia asked nervously as she got into the cockpit of the jet.

"Just stay with me and you will be fine." Tristen replied after a small pause as he strapped himself into the seat.

As Mia strapped herself securely into her seat, she examined the controls and realized they were similar to the star racers that Tristen and his team had built. Once she placed the helmet on her head, Mia then began to click the switches and nobs like she learned how to do with the racer and the engines began to roar. Smiling to herself, she steered the jet towards the bay doors as they opened to the darkness of space. Thousands of soldiers jets and other space equept machines in order to head into the fight that was coming towards them from the five enemy ships. Comunications were activated to insure that they could give and recive orders form all ten Arcs.

"Alright you cold-blooded bastards." Mia roared with anger. "You interupted my plans of getting laid tonight. So now, you all die."

"Are you serious?" Tristen laughed over the microphone in the helmet. "That is what you are mad about out of everything else?"

"Oh god, you can hear me?"

"We can all hear you little lady." A male pilot replied in her ear.

"Well that is embarrassing. Forget I said anything."

"NO can do." Tristen laughed. "Now I know your weakness and can mess with you later."

"Oh fine, whatever. Let's just kill these freaks and get on with our lives."

One by one, the fighter jets exploded from Arcs One through Ten and made their way to the five enemy ships who had released their fighters as well. Thousands of enemy ships came at them at full speed shooting lasers and plasma cannons without giving an edge. The enemy fighters were as green as the battleships that they came from, but were shapped like meteors the size of a human jet. The humans fired upon the enemy in response as the two massage armies collided into a full-on battle in space. Jets on both sides exploded with every shot with the space around them lighting up like fireworks on the Fourth Of July.

"What kind of bullets are we firing at them?" Mia asked in supprise as she took out three more enemy fighters.

"Those are the bullets that your brother and Aaron designed together." Tristen replied.

"That's right." Aaron announced over the com-system. "I decoded a small percentage of the message they sent us three years ago. It wasn't much, but it was enough to get past their shields at least. Plus we were also able to use the codes to create artifical gravity and hyperspace travel."

"Very nice. So, you can hear me to then?" Mia asked.

"More than we wanted to little sis." Vance replied.

"Oh God. Is mom and dad…"

"We are here to." Molly finished.

"How old are you Eagle Seven?" A female pilot frm Eagle Five asked over the system.

"I'm eighteen and this is my graduation day." Mia replied in an irritated manor.

"What!?" Eagle Two shouted. "We have a baby with us?"

"I am NO baby. Now can we drop it and focus on the battle please?"

Not another word was spoken as they charged into battle taking out several more enemy fighters and heading towards one of the four smaller ships. The mouth of the mothership began to open once more and started to charge its primary weapon for another attack. The laser shifted itself and aimed its deadly attack towards Arc Ten just as it did to Arc five only moments ago. A flash of light blinded all fighter jets within the perimiter and shot its second primary attack into the face of the unexpected Arc. Just like the last attack, Arc Ten emploded within seconds extingishing the lives of yet another ten persent of humanity.

"Five minutes!" Aine announced over the com-system. "We only get five minutes in between each of their primary attack. We have to destroy that laser somehow. There is no way to avoid it so we have to get rid of it. We still have thirdy minutes until the hyperdrive and engines are charged enough for the jump. That means we could lose another six ships befor then. We can't let this happen!"

"Aine," Waya said suddenly as he touched her sholder. "I'm going out there."

"What!?" Aine freaked. "No, you're not!"

"Anie, I led the Angels when I was in the Air Force and ran special forces on the ground. If anyone can take out that primary weapon, it's my team."

"But if..." She trailed off and looked at the countdown of the next attack. "You won't make it to that ship by the time it fires that laser again. We will lose another ship. Make it count within the next eight minutes before a fourth ship takes a blow."

"Right, I'll be back in twelve minutes tops."

She threw her arms around him tightly and tears began to fall down her face without caring who witnessed it. "Come back to me." She whispered in his ear and kissed his lips.

Waya released her and put his headset on as he rushed out the door of the Captain's Bridge. "Angels! Prepare for battle!"

"Roger that Commander Aholoke, Sir!" several voices resonded.

"Three of us are engaging the enemy now." A female voice announced. "We will look for a weakness in the mothership's defences and report by the time you make it to your fighter Commander."

"Roger that. Eagles, give them a hand until I get there." Waya was now in the bay and running towards his jet, which was already fueled and ready for him.

"Roger!" Tristen replied. "Let's give them some cover Eagles!"

Tristen and Mia lead the battle as they charged into the incoming enemy fighters and taking out dozens of them before catching the site of one of the four smaller battle ships. As they approched the first ship, a miniature version of the mothership's primary weapon shot out a laser and sent a shockwave through Eagles Twelve and Twenty. They zoomed past the floating rubble of the fallen jets as they spewed bullets at the massive ship to no avail. The bullets bounced off of the ship with ease as they swooped around to try a different approch by aiming their attenion at the weapons mounted atop and sides of the ship. The Eagles took out two lasers from their roots and swooped around the back as a group and began firing at the hind engines in sequince. When the bullets had no effect on the three engines, four Eagles swooped around and fired a single missile a piece. The result raved cheers as the city-sized ship exploded and lit up the darkness of space like a supernova.

As the cheers subsided, the Eagles regrouped at the same time that thousands of fighter jets spewed from the eight remaining Arcs like a swarm of angry hornets. The four remaining enemy ships returned the threat by mimicking their own swarm of deadly fighters into the now heated battle that was only minutes long. A full battle commenced as hundreds of fighter from both sides poped like bulbs against concrete with Tristen and Mia, once again, leading the assult. In perfectly timed sequence, thousands of fighter jets launched missiles at the roots of the mothership's primary weapon in hopes of stopping it. But it was no use, for the missiles had emploded before they could reach their target due to the massive electrical current that surrounded the laser cannon.

A blinding light emerged from the mouth of the mothership, sending another shockwave laser and putting a devistating end to Arc Eight. Shaking off the horror, the fighters sent out a series of missiles at the roots of the primary weapon. But the attack had no effect, for the material that the cannon was made of was too strong. At that moment, Waya Aholoke shot out of the bay of Arc One in a calm rage as he made his way towards the devistating battle. Aine had been right, he thought to himself, he would not make it before a thried ship was taken out. But he knew that it would not stop him from striking down the horrible weapon and doing his part in taking down the mothership for good.

CHAPTER 18

Knowing that Arc One would most likely be the the next target, Arcs Three, Four, Six, Seven, and Nine maneuvered themselves so that they were in front of their leading Arc like a wall. They had twenty-five minutes left before a jump could be secessfully made, but within that time, five more ships would be obliderated. Ronny had a plan on how to destroy the enemy's primary weapon, but would need Aine's approval in order to carry it out. It was a crazy and dangerouse plan, but he thought to himself that it may be the only thing that would work at this point. He would have to think fast and get Aine into a privet video call in order to lay out his desperate plan.

"I need to get ahold of Aine Aholoke in a privet chat." Ronny said quietly to a woman in communications. "Could you make this possible? It's extreamly ergent."

"Right away sir." The woman replied as she began to patch him through.

"Madam President?" A man in communications called out and Aine approched. "There is a privet meeting requested by Captain Ronny Davis."

"Patch him through." Aine replied knowing that he may have a plan.

"Aine," Ronny sighed. "We need to talk."

"You have a plan to take out that weapon or the ship itself?"

"To take out the weapon, yes. Aaron is working on a way to find an internal weakness to the mothership. The weapon is our best chance at this point."

"Understood. What exactly do you have in mind?"

"You're not going to like it, but here we go."

During Aine and Ronny's meeting, Ava and Naya took Hope and Noah back to their units while Aaron stayed behind in order to hack

"I need a favor." Aaron announced as he rushed up to Ronny.

"Let me guess." Ronny mused. "You have a plan, right?"

"I do, but I need a small piece of that laser we just destroyed. It's a long shot, but I'm thinking that if I can log into a piece of it, I can decode their system the same way I did three years ago. This way I can get us a map of the mothership and a way inside."

"Waya ask to get inside, didn't he?"

"Yes, but only because of the damage that the nuke had done to the first laser. From the inside, we may be able to destroy the entire ship. This way we can fully say goodbye to that laser and take out the last three ships easier."

"I agree, I'll contact the Eagles and have them snatch a piece before they fire upon us again. How much time would you need to get in the system?"

"Not long." Aaron said with pride. "Once I have a piece of that tech, I can get us in within the next attack."

"Very well."

<hr>

In the midst of battle, the Eagles group were given the order to retreive a shard of the primary laser from the rubble near the mothership. Mia and Tristen swarmed their enemies as they made a path to the mouth of the Reptilian battleship. They knew they were safe enough from the primary laser for another four and a half minutes to secure a shard of the demolished weapon and take it back to Arc Two. Reptilian after Reptilian hounded after them as they neard their target and each one fell like the last with ease. The new weapons that they had created from the message codes had opened many doors into future wars within intersteller travel that would insure their survival.

With the rubble in sight, Tristen swooped in and cluched a shard of the destroyed laser with the missile holder claw. The shard was about the size of his forarm with jagged edges and small eletrical currents flowing through it gaiving it a slight blue color. Once it was safly secure in the claw, it was lifted into the hatch of the jet and closed behind the doors just under the jet's bow. With their mission as a success, and three minutes to deliver it to Aaron, the Eagles broke free of the surrounding enemies and clear a path to safety. They knew that their enemy may not care if their own people were to get caught in any attack that they launch in order to take them out, so retreating with brute force was a necessity.

With two minutes to spare, Tristen docked in the bay of Arc Two as the three smaller ships began to maneuver themselves into a triangular position in front of the mothership's laser. What first looked like an attempt to protect their primary weapon from another attack, soon turned into an attack itself. A thick pole the size of a skyscraper in diameter extended from each of the three ships and connected to the mothership's laser in unison. Once the three poles were completely connected to the primary weapon, another skyscraper sized pole extended from the middle where the mothership's laser use to be. A giant red ball the size of a football dome formed at the end of the extended structure and began to glow a crimzen red color with eletrical energy.

"Dear God." Ronny murmured under his breath. Move! Move! Everyone scramble and get the second nuke to destroy that thing!"

"How long will it take you to hack that thing?" Aine aske Aaron as he took the shard of the laser from Tristen.

"Give me five minutes" Aaron promised as he sat into his computer chair.

"Make it three. We are about to lose more than one Arc from the size of that attack. We need to menuver out of the firing range as much as possible now!"

"I'll lead the next nukular attack to take out that laser Madam President." Tristen suluted her.

"I'm counting on the Eagles. The second nuke is already set up and the pilot is awaiting you to lead him."

With that, Tristen sprinted out of the Captain's Bridge and rushed into the elevator as Aaron typed furiously. He had the laser shard hooked up to Arc One's main computer with a USB attachment that he had created for this perpose. For years he had been the smartest person in all his classes and was bullied for his accomplishments. But he had found solitude in video games, comic books, and even anime throughout his childhood and adult life. Though a lot of people loved super hero movies, they laughed at him for thinking that he could be just as adaptable as they were.

But he knew they were arrogent and wrong about brain power because there were several superheroes who were made from brain power that he had looked up to. He had always wanted to be like them and use technology to his advatage to accomplish what he desired and to help the world, though saving it may have been out of reach at the time. His favorate heroes were Reed Ritchards knows as Mr. Fantastic who built many kinds of tech that had helped the world. And also Tony Stark known as Iron Man who created the suit that had made him a hero in the world's eyes. Aaron knew that he could do the same as they did if he kept learning and challenging himself in the field of technology.

This is were he had met Ava when he had went to collage for computer programing to build his own super computers. She had come to him for his support with his skills around computers and other tech like it. Though they did not plan on it, their time together had made them fall in love and she had seen the hero within him even before the message that had threatened their species survival. She had even been patient with his work when it had kept him away for hours or even days at a time. She had wanted him to succeed and did everything she could to give him the time and space to accomplish his goals.

His chance had come to help the human race and she had stood by hiss side without a second thought or arrgument against it. He types at extrodenary speed as the laser's codes flooded his computer screen just as fast. The laungage had startaled him at first, but had learned that the native tongue of Germany. He had learned the laungage in order to create the tech that they now had, and now he was reading it fluently as she scrolled through line after line of codes. Aaron had drowned everyone out around him so that he could concentrate on his work, though he knew they were shouting out commands.

Tristen and the nukular escort shot out of Arc One's bay with fierce determanation in their mission to destroy the new super weapon that threatens to wipe them out in one fell swoop. The blood red eletrical energy current flowed rapidly to the bulb at the end of the laser and like up the darkness with a hellish glow. If death, dispare, and hoplessness had a color, this would be it and the thought of extintion left a bad taste in humanity's mouth like they had ate something that had gone bad weeks prior. Suddenly, the light shone brighter and the shadow of death crosses over humanity as the atomic laser shot out its massive shockwave and sending out screams of horror through every Arc. The result was devastating as it wiped out Arcs Three, Four, and Nine like they were swipped out of the night sky like buzzing flies causing an annoyance.

The laser began to subside as Tristen made his way into battle with his small nuke team while dodging the rubble from the three Arcs. But they were flying right into trouble as the three smaller battleships detached themselves from the mothership while it was charging for it's own attack. Eagle five shot the second nuke just as the laser past by them heading straight towards Arc One. Arcs Two and Seven menuvered themselves in front of Arc One to protect their President as the Nuke connected with Mothership's primary weapon. The shockwave from the nuke caused the closest small battleship to fulter and gave the Angles their chance to release their missiles and obliderate the enemy ship.

Three enemy ships were left now that they only had two battleships along side the mothership. But celebrations would not come so soon for there were two major problems ahead. The first problem was that the mothership had released its primary laser once again and began ejecting its third and probably final laser. This sent shockwaves of fear through the three remaining Arcs knowing that they only had one nuke left and that it could only be used for destroying the mothership. The second problem was that the mothership's laser had wiped out Arc Seven as it passed in front of Arc One and slightly brushed the side of Arc Two making it fulter. But then in Mia's eyes, a third problem emurged as Tristen's jet began to spin out of control while trying to dodge the laser's energy.

"PULL UP!" Mia shouted.

"I'm trying." Tristen answered with a panic.

"PULL UP! PULL UP! PLEASE TRISTEN, PULL UP!" Mia cried with tears streaming down her cheeks like rapids in a river.

CHAPTER 19

Tristen's life flashed before his eyes as he watch the laser getting closer and closer while trying to avoid the inpact. The last three years of his life was with Mia and was the happiest that he had been and wouldn't change it for the world. But a slight chill went up his spine as time seemed to slow down to where he could see every bullet and missile being shot while he thought about what had happened less than five minutes ago while he was rushing back to his jet. While he was returning to battle after delivering the broken piece of laser to Aaron to examine, he encountered someone, or something that he could not explain. This single event made him question everything he knew and every choice he may or may not make in his or Mia's lives.

"Tristen Reevs." A small quite voice announced in an eco that seemed to be spoken in his head. "A word please?" Tristen stopped dead in his tracks and peered around to see a mist-like vision and froze.

"Who…. What are you?" Tristen replied in trebbling voice to the shodowy figure that seemed to have gold colored pupels.

And just as fast as he was placed into that flashback, he was then back to reality of the laser just in front of him. The crimzen light was blinding to him as he thought about eveything that had happened in his life that had led to this. Tristen looked in every direction and then at Mia's jet and saw her crying and screaming, though he couldn't hear her over the buzzing in his ears. He then looked back at the laser and took a deep breath as he began to accept his undeniable fate. The last words he had said before the energy cosumed him were calm and full of pure emotion.

"I'm sorry Mia." He murmured suddenly and she froze from the simple words. "I love you. I always have and Always will. We shall meet again in the abyss. Goodbye." He choked the last word out in a sudden cry as the laser hit him dead-on and demoloshing his jet.

"TRISTEN!" Mia shouted in tears. "NOOOOOO! GOD NO!"

"Move, move, move!" Eagle One shouted in command. "We have to protect the last two Arcs!"

Mia was unable to move as she stared at the dismantled remains of Tristen's fighter jet floating in the cold vacuum of space. Her puples were unnatually dilated and as black as coal, unlike her normal light green eyes she had had her entire life. The only thoughts she had in her mind was a wimpering 'no please no' even though the evidence was clear that Tristen had been lost in battle and that there was no bringing him back. Her jet was styill and floating in space much like the remains of the love of her life's jet. There hadn't even been any site of the remains of his body from what she could see.

⸺⸺◈◆◈◆◈⸺⸺

Arc Two had suffered damage to two of its three engines and was now facing another direction. It was still in front of Arc One, but the sieds were facing Arc One and the enemy mothership to make their main ship unseen. Ronny had exited the captain's bridge and rushed down the hall to Naya and her kids' unit so he could get them to safty. Mini explosions waved through the Arc like small shockwaves that made the lights flicker and other electronics short circuit from the damage. He passed multiple civiliens that were running around in a panic as they made their way to the escape pods that were located in every section of the Arc.

Several locations on the Arc were sealed off by blast doors making people, including Ronny, have no other choice but to find other ways around. He had made it to Naya's unit just as a small explosion went off in the upstairs of her unit where the bedrooms were located. In a panic, he sprinted towards the door and unlocked it with his personal override cardkey and pushed the door in with great force. Smoke filled the unit like thick fog on an early morning lake making it impossible to see two feet in front of him. Goosebumps of pure fear spread across his body.

"Jason, Arial!?!" Naya shouted as Ronny spotted her. "Where are you?"

"Mom!" Jason replied with a shout as he came down the stairs carrying his sister. "The blast knocked her out."

"Lets get you three into an escape pod." Ronny sujested as he rushed up to them.

"Ronny!" Naya cheered and hugged him tightly. "Thanks for coming for us."

"Like I would every leave you three alone in a situation like this." Ronny teased with a smile. "Now let's get out of here."

Ronny rushed down the hall to the elevators with an unconscious Arial in his arms with Jason and Naya running on both sides of him. Multiple mini explosions filled the hall as they reached the elevators and pressed the button for the third floor. When they arrived on the third floor, Ronny led them to the closest escape pod and opened the hatch. Outside the widows, multiple pods were being ejected from th Arc along side the others from the destroyed Arcs. Each pod was similer in looks and size of a travel bus and could hold up to three hundred people compfertably.

The seats were cushioned and were equipt with full body seatbelts to insure that each passenger was safe doing launch. Outside the Arc, multiple pods were activating their hyperdrives and launching into several different directions from the battle. Ronny and Naya teamed up to strap Jason and Arial, who was still unconscious, into their seats. The front of the pod had a control panel that streached the length of the pod with two seats for pilots. Once the kids wer safely strapped in, Ronny helped Naya secure herself in one of the pilot seats.

"Okay, listen to me very carfully." Ronny said calmly.

"Okay, I trust you." Naya replied with a nervous smile.

"I'm going o get Ava and Hope so I can take them to the bridge. Arial is unconscious and can't travel there at this time so stay here for now and I'll come back for you when I can. If an explosion disconnects you from the ship, pull down on the red and yellow lever then push it in to activate the hyperdrive and get yourselves out of here."

"But that will send us in a different direction." Naya pointed out, still with trust in her voice.

"I know it will, and many others are doing the same. If this happens, I will find you. I promise."

"Okay, I trust you. Thank you for everything." With a slight nod, Ronny turned away and closed the pod's hatch as he left and raced towards Ava's unit.

"Got it!" Aaron yelled as Ronny, Ava, and Hope entered the bridge.

"Can you get past their defences?" Ronny asked as he rushed up to him without skipping a beat.

"Much better than that." Aaron replied proudly as he typed furiously at his computer. "I hacked into their mainframe and foud schematics to the mothership. We can use the map and head straight to the core with the A-bomb and put an end to this battle. We can enter o the bay just to the right of the ship. That is the closest enterance."

"Madam president," Ronny announced. "Did you catch all of that?"

"Yes I did." Aine replied. "And I'm sending my forces now. Thank you Aaron."

"Just doing my job." We still have five minutes before we can safely jump and five minutes before the mothership's next strike."

"Then we have five minutes to end this battle." Aine murmured.

"Then I will head out and get as many citizens on Arc Two to safty while you end this battle." Everyone agreed and the final coutdown began.

Mia floated through the battle like she was nothing more than a fallen warrior with enemies and allies zooming past her without a second glance. As far as everyone knew, she was already dead and not worth anyone's concern with death spewing everywhere. Then she overheard the conversation with Ronny and Aaron and that jolted her back to reality as her eyes going as dark as the space around her. The only words that formed in her mind as she sperd the jet back to life was 'kill, kill, revenge, revenge'. Now that she had a way to deliver just that, she raced towards Arc One in order to gain what was needed to carry out the task of revenge.

Her mind was blank and only focused on the one task that would stay in her mind until it was complete or she died in the process. Once Mia had reached Arc One, she landed roughly in the docking bay before slaming open the hatch and jumping to the ground. Several pilots and medical staff met ner as she made her way towards the jet with the A-bomb, but she just pushed them aside without a second thought. 'Kill, kill, revenge, revenge' kept playing over and over as she reached her desired jet and ame face to face with the pilot that was intended to fly it. He halted her with a stiff arm but she was deaf to all sounds other than the words that repeated themselves over and over in her mind.

She looked up at him with coal black eyes that seemed to not have any whites anywhere and scawled at him. The moment that he put an arm on her sholder to calm her down, she thrusted an elbow up into his bulky neck and sent him to his knees. Without hesitation, she pushed passed him as several people rushed at her and yelling for her to stop. But she was still deaf to all commands and she buckaled herself up and closed the hatch just as the other pilots reached her jet. She ignighted the engine and pushed forward making everyone having to jump to the side in order to avoid getting run over. She shot the jet out of the docking bay as fast as lightning with the A-bomb intact and revenge on her mind.

"Mia!" Molly demanded. "Answer me damn it! Wake up!"

"What the hell is she doing?" Aine demanded in a frantic tone.

"She gets like this when she blacks out. She has no control over her actions until she wakes up. We can't reach her until she wakes up and calms down."

"Doesn't look like that is going to happen anytime soon. Either way, she needs tro hear the orders because we don't have time for soeone to switch out the ships. We need to protect her."

"You heard the President," Eagle One announced. "Let's cover that girl's ass and get this battle over with."

"Four minutes." Aine replied. "We have four minutes to destroy that ship or we are all dead."

Mia, still in a blacked-out daze, was surrounded by the remander of the Eagles and Angels groups in an arrow formation in an attempt to cut through the enemy lines. Vance had made his way to the group from Arc One side by side with Waya Aholoke to help support the infiltration mission. The massive group of fourty fighter jets blasted through enemy ships with war crys and determination. Vance was the first to cut from the group as he created a path straight through the middle of the on-coming enemies. He was fully loaded and ready to lay down his life so that humanity could survive and learn of their first inersteller war.

He zig-zagged through every reptilian fighter with his specially made bullets while saving his missiles for the internal battle. He ripped through the hoard of enemies with ease as a cut a path straight to the bay on the right side of the mothership. Three enemy fighters rushed him as he looped around and blasted through them in a single line before zooming past the rubble. The path to the mothership was now clear and ready for the main fight to begin as Vance lead the team toward the bay doors. But suddenly they had begun to close giving the impression that the enemy knew what they were trying to do and were making an attempt to stop them.

Ronny rushed through the severely damaged Arc Two as he lead the surviving citizens from the housing unit floors to nearby escape pods. Tiny explosions made many people scream and panic, but Ronny had kept them calm as they filled up pod after pod. After filling up each pod, he gave them instructions on how to launch them and activate hyperdrive. Throughout his life, he had done more to help others than he did to help himself because he had grown up with more than he thought that he desurved. This made him want to give to those who had little or nothing which made him feel like he earned everything he had or ever will have in his life.

Ronny and his family were never ritch, but they always had everything that they needed and considered comfortable. Growing up, he watched as other people struggled and he wondered if there was a way he could one day help others. After high school he had noticed just how overpopulated that the world was and that people were killing the enviernment in order to gain land and materials so that they could make money. Greed caused a lot of people to suffer so that some could live great lives and think that the world was fine as it was. Though he had disagreed with these things, he knew that humanity at least had the choice in their own distruction.

Now the entire race was being slaughtered and humanity was on the verge of extinction by those who chose to take that right from them. Ronny made his way back towards the bridge after securing the citizens who were trapped in the damaged parts of the Arc into escape pods. Those who were in the functioning parts of the Arc, he made sure they were safely huddled down in their units until they launched into hyperspace. As of three years ago, hunanity was no longer tied to ritch olr poor, nor were they clinging on to greediness. Now they were clinging onto their right to exsist and Ronny had his chance to do something worth while for everyone.

Mia thrashed her way through the enemy's docking bay in the path that Vance had cleared for the nuke team just seconds before. Enemy fighters rushed her just as she entered their domain, but she was too angry to be consumed by fear. Instead, she lashed out in anger as she blasted through reptilian after reptilian in a rage weather they were in a fighter jet or on the ground running, she did not care. All she saw was red, and not just their blood, and could only hear the words 'kill' and 'revenge' ringing in hefr ears. But one thig did come through toher, though she did not answer, was the voice of Aaron as he gave her directions in her ear.

"Mia, listen!" Aaron chimed in. "You will need to fight your way through a four-mile long highway then turn left."

She stayed silent as several enemy fighters surrounded her and her team from every direction while they made their way down the long highway. Mia was still in the lead as she slaughtered every ship and creature that she laid eyes on without any remorse. She dodged every oncoming attack as she returned fire with her team of fighters close behind giving her support. The hallway was the size of Hollywood blvd. with massive structures on both sids with enough room for everyone to menuver around the long battlefeild.

Every structure has alien reptiles perched on landing and shooting at the nuke team as they passed by like lightning bolts.the nuke team zig-zagged around the structures and dodging their attacks with Mia still in front leading the deadly assault. She used every skill tghat Tristen had taught her the past three years about flying and shooting. Even through her blind rage, she never faltered or lost control of the jet as she whipped through mothership and turned left at the end of the long hallway.

"Good," Aaron sighed. "You're actually listening. At least I know I can lead you through the ship. But the next section is tricky and concentration is needed to secceed. You will have to zigzag through the structures, which I would guess will bw swarming with enemies, unti you reach, what will lookm like a small town-sized structure in the middle. Inside that structure is where the core of the mothership is."

"I take back what I said about having a baby on out team." A familiar female voice came over the radio.

"Not bad for a street racer." Vance added.

"She's a what!? No wounder she is good at drifting."

"Vance, watch after your sister." Waya chimed in. "The rest of you land here with me so we can keep this section clear for when we make our escape."

"Just be carefull." Aine replied with worry in her voice.

Once Mia and Vance were out of sight, Waya and the rest of the pilots landed near the enterance of the city-sized room as hundreds of reptilians crowded around them. The soldiers bared their arms and the first ground battle had begun with Waya leading the front lines. Weapons of all shapes, sizes, and types blasted through one another with both sids taking casualties. The Native American blood ran hot in Waya's vains as he took down his enemies with both his AK-47 and bare hands. He had always been a great fighter with all different kinds of weapons and hand to hand combat that led him up the ranks in the military. The battle raged as Mia zigzagged through the massive ship in search of the core so it could be destroyed.

Aine focused on maintaining the remaining two Arcs as the time dwindled down with only two and a half minutes to go before the next primary attack would wipe them out. With her leadership, the thousands of pilots outside were able to take down the third reptilian battleship making only two ships left. One more small battleship and the mothership was all that remained as the human fighter jets swarmed around the small reptilian ship and began pumbling it with their remaining missiles. With a massive explosion that could cause the earth to quake, the final reptilian battleship exploded like a nova star and lit up the darkness and shed a light of hope upon humanity. Aine then slid down the railling of the stairs and connected with Arc Two in hopes that they were alright.

"Status report." Aine murmured.

"Everyone is either safe in their units, or jumping into hyperspace in the escape pods." Ronny replied.

"And our hyperdrives?"

"Almost there." Aaron replied in haste. "Less than a minute to charge. That meant they have two minute to destroy that ship and get back to the Arcs."

"Then it's time for everyone to begin retreating and leave the rest to Mia and the nuke team." Ronny announced.

"I agree." Aine replied. "Call everyone back."

While Ronny and Aine called for a retreat, Aaron continued to type furriously on the computer as the hyperdrive charge was nearing the minimum eighty-five percent for launch. Ava sat beside him with hope in her arms, who was sleeping through the entire battle. Aaron switched between computers as he watched Mia and Vance's progress at the same time that he increased the charge of the hyperdrive. Everyone stopped what they were doing and stared at Aaron in awe and envy of his skills with technology. They knew he was the one who had created the super computers that they were running and created the codes that made it possible for them to enter hyperdive for the first time in human history.

"Got it!" Aaron shouted, but then shrunk down in his seat when he realized that he was being watched. "Um… Hyperdive is ready."

"Then let's get everyone inside and get out of here." Aine ordered. "end that ship and let's go!"

<hr>

Mia fought through the multiple attacks thrown at her as she edged closer to her destination. Enemy fighters swooped in as she dodged and Vance took them out so that they wouldn't waste time looping around. Massive alien tanks that were shaped like dung beetles shot plasma cannons at them as the large dome-shaped structure came into view. They menuvered out of the way and shot their own missiles back at them without skipping a beat. Desperate to defend the ship's core, several reptilians took ahold of the turrents in the windows of the structure and shot multiple plasma cannons.

With only a minute and a half before the next attack on the Arcs, Mia and Vance looped around the dome structure in hopes of finding a safe way in. But the massive structure was protected on all side by torrents that shot at them at every turn. Mia's impatience got the better of her and she launched her final two regular missiles and blasted open her own enterence to the core. Her and Vance zipped into the man-made hole and came face to face with a skyscraper-sized green and white energy vibrating with immense power. The energy pulsed out waves of power sending a rumble through their jets as they lessend the distance.

"Okay Mia," Aaron announced. "All you have to do is launch the A-bomb straight at the center of the core and get the hell out of their. The bomb will be set to go off within a minute of the launch and should be enough time to retreat since Waya and his team cleared a path for you."

Mia did as she was instructed and launched the A-bomb straight into the center of the core when she was only two feet away from it. The nuke crackled as it cut through the massive energy sorce while she zoomed passed it heading in the opposite direction in which she came. She shot through the walls and made her way to the mothership's bridge to carry out one more piece of revenge. Vance followed her in a desperate attempt to stop her, but his pleas never reached her ears. A chain reaction from the nuke and the core colliding and pulsed rappidly as the nuke's countdown dwindled to zero and emploded.

CHAPTER 20

In one of the escape pods, Naya sat strapped into the pilot seat awaiting a signal from the captain's bridge. She could hear the shouts from the other pods and watched as some of them launched into space and then into hyperspace. Jason sat diagonal from her holding his unconscious sister's head in his lap while they were also strapped into their seats. It had been a long three years and she had learned a lot about her children that she hadn't known before. They were more like their father than she had realized because they had begun to chage after his death.

Naya felt as if she needed to spend more time with them alone, but she knew that she couldn't abandon Ronny's kindness that he had shown since her husband's death. He was like family to her and wouldn't know how to go about telling him that she needed time with just herself and her kids. She knew that he would understand, but with everything that had happened the past three years, she hadn't had the heart to tell him. That's when she had desided that when they landed wherevere they were headed, she would sit down with him and explain how she felt. She knew his heart was in the right place and that he blamed himself for what happened to her husband, but she had to put him at ease bay telling him that he had done more than enough and that she could make it on her own from now on.

While holding his sister's head in his lap, Jason noticed that Arial's skin began to get moist and gain a red-tint glow. Before he could let his mother know what was happening, there was a massive explosion that had forced their pod to eject from the Arc. Naya braced herself as the pod swerled around the empiness of space with force enough to bounce them off the walls if they hadn't been strapped into their seats. Naya and Jason yelled in a panic until the pod stopped spinning and began to float calmly. They could see Arc's One and Two outside the window as the battle ragged on and seemed like it would never end. Naya turned to see if her kids were alright and nothiced that Arial was still out cold and the red tint to her now glowing skin.

"Are you two okay?" Naya asked in a husky voice.

"Arial is glowing mom." Jason replied.

"Jason, you're starting to glow as well. I thought it was from the explosions, but you both are actually glowing." Naya unstrapped herself and rushed to them both.

"I… I don't feel so good mom." Jason said weakly.

"I'll get some help. I'll call Ronny." But then Jason had passed out as well. "Jason! Arial! God you both need a doctor." Naya looked back at the cockpit and then back at her children and closed her eyes tight with a nervous sigh. "Sorry Ronny, I'll see you again some day.

Naya tightend up Jason and Arial's straps and rushed back the the pilot seat and strapped herself in. She then grabbed the red and yellow lever and pulled down before hesitating for just a second. She quickly looked back at her kids and then the still battling Arcs before turning back to the lever in her hand. Taking a deep breath, she pushed the lever in and activated the hyperdrive that caused the control panael to light up and an alarm to go off. Multiple colors began to form out the windshield and the escape pod jerked forward as a hole opened up, sending the pod through the hole and away from the battle.

"Sir, another escape pod entered hyperspace." A man from intel announced.

"Which one?" Ronny asked.

"Pod 563 sir."

"Naya, Jason, Arial. I'll gind you. I promise." Ronny whispered. "What's the status on our hyperdrive?"

"It stopped charging sir, the engines are too damaged. But President Aholoke said that they are charged enough for one jump."

"Can we jump with the engines this damaged?"

"Yes, but I don't know how far we would get with one engine sir."

"That's fine. Contact Arc One." Communications connected with Arc One just as the reptilian mothership began to selfdestruct.

"Captain Davis." Aine smiled pleased. "It's good to see that you're alright."

"Likewise." Ronny replied. "I'm also glad to see that the mothership plan was a seccess. I hope the pilot is alright as well."

"She is in the process of heading toward the mothership's bridge. She is… in a rage at the moment."

"As I've been told. Quite a firecracker, that one."

"I take it that you have news. I hope it's not bad news."

"It just depends on on what you consider good or bad."

"Even in all this chaos, you still have jokes. Mr. Davis."

"If I die. I want to die the same way I lived." Ronny smiled.

"Don't we all. So what is your news?"

"Our engines are too damaged to get into formation. We can still jump although, we can only jump from this position."

"I see." Aine sighed. "Do whatever you need to do. Just try and contact me when you get where your going."

"Will do, as soon as we find tech that is powerful enough."

"See you soon Captain Davis."

"You to madam president." When the screen went black, Ronny turned toward the Arc Two pilots. "Punch it into hyperdrive and let's get the hell out of here."

"Aye sir." Bothe pilots said in unison.

The pilots sounded an alarm through Arc Two that warned the passengers that they were about to enter hyperspace. Withing a few short moments, everyone was safely buckled down and braced themselves for the jump. Both pilots pulled down on the hyperdrive levers and pushed them in at the exact same time. Arc Two jolted forward as a rainbow colored hole began to open up for everyone to witness. Chunkes of Arc Two broke off as it sped up and disappeared into the hole in the dead of space and left the battle behind them.

Mia zigzagged through the mothership in a rage as the core exploded behind her and sent out shockwaves in every direction. The reptilian enemies around her didn't bother trying to kill her for they were trying to escape the doomed ship in a panic. They all zipped past her in the opposite direction heading towards the area in which Waya and his team were now retreating the docking bay. Mia's family yelled into the headset for her to retreat, but she was too blinded by rage to listen or reply. Instead, she sped towards theh mothership's bridge to kill the captain that had ordered the attack in which ended Tristen's life. She blasted through the walls as she neared her destination and came face to face with the monstrous captain of the reptilian fleet.

The green scaly beast stood tall as he whipped his tail in rage from what the human had done to his ship. He knew that the mission was a failure because he had counted at least a hundred escape pods that had entered hyperspace ad escaped. The mission was to extinguish the the human race in its entirety, but that had been a failure from the first escape pod. He had ordered the triple assult laser to finish off the Arcs, but many had stood strong and killed a coutless number of his soldiers. He knew hi would die not only because of his ship exploding, but because he also let an Arc slip into hyperspace and would be killed for his insolence even if he would survive the battle.

The reptilian beast caught Mia's eyes in a staredown as she slammed through the hole in the bridge that she had shot open. The monster whipped his tail as he used his powerful hind legs to jump onto the window of her jet. She openend the hatch as they both sped toward the bridge window leading to space and the gigantic lizard learched inside as she stood up. The hatch closed at the jet smashed through the window into the vacuum of space and the two rageful creatures stared at each other only inches apart. The head of the eight foot tall lizard leaned against the window of the jet as he snarled down at her.

"You destroyed my ship!" The reptilian hissed.

"You killed my boyfriend." Mia snapped back. "On my planet, they call that an eye for an eye."

"You should have laid down and died like the abominations you are."

"The only abominations are you cold-blooded freaks. Besides, we humans don't know how to give up." Mia's eyes grew darker and darker as she slipped back into the mindless being she was duing the mothership's invasion. "Now, befor I kill you and my people dissect your body, anything you would like to say?"

"Th...those eyes...." The reptilian faltured. "You can't... this can't.... we are superior to you humans!"

"I'll show you superior, you freak!"

He shook the dazed look off of his face and lunged at her in anger, but she pulled off a split in order to dodge him. She then swirled around and jumped onto his back as he flailed and hissed in a rage of bering touched. She reached down to her combat boots and pulled out her huner's knife and twisted it around in her fingers as she jabbed it at her enemy's throat. Before he could fully react, the knife slashed open a large gash on the side of his neck and jerked Mia off his back and stumbled backwards. Without losing a step, Mia twisted around and jabbed the knife at her opponent with the success of lunging the blade deep into this throat and twisting sideways.

The reptilian captain fell to the floor of the jet dead at Mia's feet and she slumped down into her seat out of breath. Hearing the explosion coming from behind her, she grabbed the controles and sped towards Arc One. Several reptilian fighers were on her tail and she looked to be the only human soldier in the area as she sped the jet up to get away. Backup soon arrived when she spotted Vance and Waya leading a team towards her as they blasted through the hoard of reptials. They flew alongside her as they entered the docking bay of Arc One with cheers surrounding their jets.

As she slowly exited her jet in exhaustion, she was met by her family's smiling faces with open arms. Finally breaking down, she fell into their arms and cried for her people that had died, her family that were still alive, and for the love that she had lost. Everyone crowded around her as she passed out in her tears and carried her off to get medical attention. It had been a long and hard faught battle, but the human race had survived their very first, but not last, inersteller war. This would be the first of many to come, but now was the time for rest and searching for the ones who had jumped from the slaughter.

"Madam President," A woman from intel announced. "Everyone is safely aboard the Arc and the hyperdrive is fully ready for the jump."

"Very well." Aine replied as she held Waya and Noah in her arms. "Make the jump. After all, we do have allies waiting for us at the Milky Way Grand Planet. And we have to regroup with those who had jumped during the battle."

As the pilots readed the Arc for hyperspace, Aine Aholoke stared out the windows in tears as she thought about the world they were leaving behind. 'Farewell Earth." Was all she could think about as the tears stung her eyes as they fell. 'Maybe we will see you again some day. Even though you were better to us than we were to you.' With those final thoughts, Arc One disappeared into the wormhole and jolted toward their next destination in the great beyond.

Printed in the United States
by Baker & Taylor Publisher Services